SECRET OF
LOST MOUNTAIN

A STORY FOR
IMAGINATIONS
OF ALL AGES

Secret of Lost Mountain

A Story for Imaginations of all Ages

Bernard Scott

Illustrated by
Ronaldo Florendo

Logos Institute Press

Published by Logos Institute Press

Other Works by the Author

Brian's Law
A Book of Short Stories

The Mystery of Work
An Anthology

ISBN 978-0-9801174-7-9 (Paperback)

http://logosinstitute.org

To Arlene

ILLUSTRATIONS

CONTENTS

CHAPTER ONE

THE FATHER'S TALE

MY NAME IS DAISY *and I wish to relate to you a story my father told me when I was very young. I tell it now that I am old because it has remained lodged in my memory to this day, a tale so remarkable I feel it must be shared before it is lost to time and the inevitable. Perhaps you will receive this story in much the way that I did, as something compelling with its own kind of beauty.*

So one night as my father put me to bed, he took my hand and said he would tell me a story. That night I asked him to tell me a different kind of story, a story about a hidden, distant land no one knew anything about, a place no one would suspect could even exist. And so he did. Hand in hand, he told me an incredible tale that came to stretch over many, many nights. How much of this story might actually be true and how much of it is just made up I do not really know, but my father told me of a people and of a circumstance so strange and yet so real I still feel their presence near me today. And now, if you will permit me, I too take your hand. I trust you'll agree the tale is very worth its telling.

A STRANGE WORLD

IMAGINE A STRANGE WORLD hidden back in the remotest mountains of a poor, distant land, a secret place with inhabitants so unusual in fact that, had word of it ever reached the civilized world, people would have scoffed. And, indeed, no one in the civilized world had the faintest notion such a thing could actually be. No idea as yet at least. But along the coast of that distant land you could hear rumors about a mysterious mountain tribe said to live deep in the interior. "Way back in the mountains" these coastlanders would say with a broad swing of the hand. Not that they necessarily believed their own words. No coastlander had ever seen these people—no coastlander ever ventured that deep into the interior— and information about this tribe was next to non-existent. Except for one thing that was always brought up and was very strange indeed. It is hard even to imagine it. When the members of this tribe speak or move about, it was said, they make no sound. If you asked coastlanders about it, the more educated simply shook their head and laughed at the notion. An entire tribe wrapped in silence made no sense to them. The less learned were not so sure. "That part of the mountains cannot be entered," they would say. "Who knows what might be up there." But the poor and unschooled had little doubt about it. Something dark is at work in those mountains, they would say. There could easily be such people up there, ghostlike souls who speak and move without sound of any kind.

Then one day in the little coastal port of this remote region, an old tramp steamer pulled up to the port's solitary pier, a rusty old vessel on its semi-annual visit bearing long-awaited cargo from across the seas, and with it sometimes the rare passenger or two, more likely than not a missionary. It was late morning when this little freighter tied up, and not long afterwards the knot of coastlanders gathered there on the pier saw a solitary passenger descend the gangway, a white man neither young nor old with strong, pleasant enough features and who turned out to be anything but a missionary.

The newcomer stood there at the foot of the gangway amidst his luggage, looking around at the unfamiliar surroundings with alert, anticipating eyes, waiting it seemed for whatever might come his way. That proved to be the port official scurrying to perform a function he only too rarely got to exercise. The port official approached the stranger and in the local *Moulawi* dialect asked for his papers, speaking extra loud in the vain hope he might be understood. The newcomer readily obliged, handing over documents that proved to be quite in order. He turned out to be friendly and to the astonishment of the port official and the idlers nearby, addressed the official in the local language. In formal but almost perfect *Moulawi,* he explained that he was not a commercial traveler nor anything like a tourist. He was in fact a scientist, an anthropologist with a deep interest in languages, and he had come on a scientific project that would shortly take him into the interior. Seeing the port official raise eyebrows at this, the stranger added that what brought him was a remarkable story he had come across back in his own land, about a mountain tribe in the remote inland mountains of this country. What was so remarkable, he said, was the claim, a rumor really, that this mysterious tribe lives in complete silence, makes no noise nor sound of any kind, not even when they speak. Perhaps the port inspector knows something about this? If the story were true, he added, it would be of considerable scientific interest to the rest of the world. The port official smirked and said nothing. "*Explorer*," he wrote down, shaking his head. As far as this official was concerned, this story was unworthy of comment.

There was little custom in this isolated coastland port for the caring of overseas visitors and soon the gathering on the pier drifted off leaving this newcomer, this so-called "explorer," alone and unattended, surrounded by his luggage. But before long a boy came up to him speaking *Moulawi*.

"I help?" he asked with a huge grin.

"Good, son," the explorer said, nodding. "I need a place to stay."

"Not problem. I find place." The boy looked to be about twelve years of age, a somewhat frail, light-skinned coastal native. "I take," the youth said, picking up two of the bags. He had already arranged for a friend with a cart to follow with the rest of the luggage.

They walked along the shore road for a quarter of a mile and then turned into a little street lined with untidy, rundown bungalows.

"This my house," the boy announced proudly, stopping before a cottage that looked like it had not been painted in generations. "Live with father," the youth said, inviting the explorer to enter. "You stay."

Inside, the father, seated in a chair with a book, looked up quizzically at the intrusion. He did not get up. In

*A rare foreigner arrives at the coastal port of a
far off, primitive land.*

rapid-fire *patois* the explorer was unable to follow, the boy explained the circumstance of their coming. The father looked the explorer over, then nodded his consent. The explorer would stay in the son's room. The son would sleep in his room, on the floor.

"You priest?" the father asked.

The explorer found that funny. "Hardly a priest," he said laughing.

"Priest stay here once," the boy interjected. "Long time ago."

"That's interesting," the explorer said, perking up. Turning to the father he asked, "Do you remember his name by any chance?"

The father shook his head. "Priest here forty years ago."

"I learned *Moulawi* from the writings of a Jesuit who was here around that time," the explorer said. "Was your priest a Jesuit?"

"Maybe Jesuit," the father said.

"It would be remarkable if he's the same man!" the explorer said, his interest spiking. "An unbelievable stroke of luck actually."

"You speak *Moulawi* like grammar book," the father said. "Not like people."

The explorer laughed. "No doubt," he said smiling. "I speak your language the way I think my language." Getting back, he asked, "Do you remember your priest's name?"

The father said nothing.

"Forty years long time," the boy said.

The explorer smiled at that and turned to the father.

"The Jesuit I learned your language from was Christopher Damian. The Reverend Father Christopher Damian, S.J." He pronounced the long, formal title as if he found it amusing. "Damian," he repeated. "Christopher Damian." Peering at the father, he asked, "Does that name mean anything? He was here in your country about the same time as this priest of yours."

"Priest die here," the father said.

"Christopher Damian?" the explorer asked, eyes widening.

The father shrugged his shoulders.

"The priest died in this house?" the explorer said.

"In room you stay in," the father said.

"Did you know him well?" the explorer asked.

"Not well," the father said.

"Can you tell me about him? Was he here with you long?"

"Not long," the father said. Turning to his son, he said, "You take him to room now."

The son did as he was told. "Father was teacher," the son said once inside his room.

"He seems not well," the explorer said.

The son nodded. "Now father only teach me. I read father's books."

"That's good," the explorer said looking around. Books were lying everywhere. Some were in the explorer's own language.

"You missionary?" the son asked.

"Do I look like a missionary?" the explorer asked, amused.

"Only missionaries come on boat," the boy said.

7

"I don't think I'm the type," the explorer said with a laugh.

"Then why you come here?" the boy asked.

"I'm on my way into the interior, up into the mountains," he said. "A research project," he added.

The boy looked incredulous. "You go on river?"

"That's my plan," the explorer said.

The boy shook his head. "River dangerous," he said.

"I'd like to talk to your father about this priest," the explorer said.

"Priest your friend?" the boy asked.

"I have no idea who either of them is," the explorer said. "But they were both here in this country about forty years ago. There's a good chance they could be the same man."

"I ask father," the boy said. Before he left, he turned and said proudly, "Father know your language. He promise he teach me."

Some time later the boy knocked on the door and invited the explorer to join him and his father for supper. The father was seated at a table. The boy, who had prepared the meal, put a plate before his father and then one for the visitor and finally one for himself. The father gestured to the explorer to join them.

"You have good son like this, too?" the father asked.

The explorer hesitated. "I do, actually," he said finally.

"And he must be about your son's age by now. A few years older maybe."

The father frowned. "What you want ask?" he said.

"This Jesuit, Father Damian, wrote some interesting

things about your country," the explorer said. "I need to learn more about him."

"You write books?" the father asked.

The explorer smiled. "I write monographs," he said, "about places and languages the world knows almost nothing about. Like your country." He added with a laugh, "I can't say many read my books."

"You write book about my country?" the father asked.

"Maybe one day, perhaps," the explorer said. "Right now it would help me to know something more about the Jesuit who stayed with you. He could be this Christopher Damian. I have a special reason for wanting to know about him"

The father regarded the explorer for a long moment. "You go up river," he said, "probably you not come back."

"Christopher Damian did not seem afraid of the river," the explorer said. "He wrote about his plans to travel up the river to the *Chiroki*. Do you know anything about them?" he asked the father. "I understand the *Chiroki* live in the hills along the river's headwaters."

The father barely nodded with a tilt of his head.

The explorer leaned over to the father and said, "It would be worth something to me to know if this Damian ever did what he planned. Did the priest who lived with you go to the *Chiroki*?"

The father said nothing, focusing back on his food, knife and fork in either boney hand.

"Any information about this priest would be invaluable to me," the explorer said. "Did your priest go on the river, do you know?" Then he added, "It would be worth something to know."

The father looked away and spoke something in the local *patois* to the son. The son leapt up and disappeared into the father's bedroom.

The explorer drew closer. "Let me tell you why I have come to your country," he said. He hesitated and then added, "It might be easier for me to tell you this in my own language, if that's OK. Your son said you taught it."

The father nodded.

The explorer smiled and began, speaking more freely now. "I teach too, at a university, that is, when I am not off in a jungle somewhere doing research. Anyway, not long ago, in our school library, I came across an old, handwritten manuscript describing the language of this region, *Moulawi*. It was written by this Jesuit, Christopher Damian. I had never heard of him but right away I could tell he was an excellent, truly gifted linguist. His manuscript described *Moulawi* in great detail, written while he was still here in your port city. It is a lovely work with exhaustive vocabulary lists, rules for grammar and pronunciation, all anyone would need to learn the language. I found his description of your language quite fascinating but that is not why I determined to learn it. That's not why I came here. At the end of his manuscript there was a little note, written in Latin oddly enough. In it this priest said that now that he had finished this work, he was going to depart the coast and go upriver to the *Chiroki,* a tribe living in the hills by the headwaters of the great river. He wrote that he knew the journey would be dangerous and that he might not return, but he felt a call to go to the *Chiroki* because no priest had ever been to them before.

"Then, curiously, this Christopher Damian wrote of another reason for wanting to face the great river. He described tales that coastlanders had often told him, stories about an unnamed tribe who lived in the mountains just beyond the *Chiroki* villages—a mysterious, isolated people who were 'lost to silence' is the way he put it, a strange tribe that lives and speaks without making a single sound, no sound of any kind. As a linguist, he wondered how such a thing could be, and he vowed, if he is able to reach the *Chiroki*, that he would go into the mountains beyond and learn what he could about this most curious rumor."

The explorer went on, "You see, like this priest Damian, I am a student of languages also. And I too wonder how such a thing can possibly be—how a tribe like that can live and speak in complete silence. So I need to know if this priest ever followed through on his plan. Did he go on the river? Did he get to the *Chiroki*? Did he learn anything about this tribe of silent people? I made inquiries in my country. No one knows what became of Christopher Damian, not even his fellow Jesuits. He just disappeared."

The explorer leaned closer to the father and, lowering his voice, confided, "I will reward anyone who can give me information about him."

The father laid his knife and fork down and called out to his son. A torrent of *patois* flowed between them through the bedroom door, and shortly the son reappeared and handed his father an old, thick, worn manila envelope. The father opened it and drew out a single sheet of paper with handwriting.

"Priest left this," the father said, handing the page over to the explorer.

The handwriting, in *Moulawi*, was faded and difficult to read, almost like scrawlings. It appeared to be a brief letter, penned by someone under considerable stress. At the top was the word *Teeku*, possibly a name, but not *Moulawi* sounding. This was followed by a barely readable single line: *"Tell Sabuknu I offer my death for them."* The signature was in worse shape, scribbled and hardly legible. The explorer had to hold the sheet up to the light, but then there it was, unmistakable, a signature that could only read *Katalan* Damian.

"My God!" the explorer exclaimed. "But this is him! Christopher Damian! This is unbelievable!" The explorer pushed the note across the table and pointed to the writing. Lapsing back now into *Moulawi*, he asked, "These word, *Teeku, Sabuknu, Katalan,* they're not *Moulawi.* Are they *Chiroki*?"

The father did not answer.

"Who is this *Teeku*?" the explorer asked, studying the letter. "The note is addressed to him. Do you know him? Did he ever see this?"

The father again said nothing.

"What did the priest tell you?" the explorer pleaded.

"Priest come down river with bad wounds," the father said. "From animal. He die soon."

"But he must have said something?" the explorer said, stretching for the father's arm and then backing off.

The father shrugged his shoulders. "I young man forty years ago, live in father's house. He not tell me."

The explorer slumped back. "Of course. That was for-ty years ago."

The father took out the remaining contents of the manila envelope, a bound sheaf of handwritten pag-es, and passed them over. Page after page was filled with lists of words. The explorer saw at once that the writing was by the same even hand of the *Moulawi* manuscript he had devoured at the university. The words were in an unfamiliar language, followed by their translation.

"These have to be *Chiroki* terms, no?" the explorer said looking up.

"Ask *Chiroki*," the father said blankly.

"Can I find *Chiroki* here on the coast?" the explorer asked.

Again the father shrugged. "Maybe look in native quarter."

"I take," the boy said grinning.

The explorer considered the father for a moment. "May I keep these papers for a while?" he said at length.

"You buy?" the father said.

The explorer smiled. "Don't worry," he said. "We'll talk about that later, all right?"

The father said nothing and picked up a book.

"May I ask you something," the explorer said. "You are a learned man. A teacher. Do you believe this story about the mountain tribe? People who live and speak in complete silence?"

The father did not look up. "It not true," he said.

"This priest Damian seemed to think there was some truth to the story," the explorer said.

asum – how

banyo – understand

bulgani – long time

buti la? – agreed?

chilani – friend

dochi – daughter

dono – but

dundi – mountain

fulana – meet

galiva – heal

hindo – son

hoda – also

Jaka – curse

ka – and

kamiso – man

kano – blue

katalan – priest

kinasi – mother

la – am, is, are, yes

lunas – berry

ladi ladi – OK, good

loki loki – hello

masi – bearer

mino – to go

miso – take

muti – gift

na – of

ni – this

nili – sweet

no, nu – I, you

o – past tense

pomago – help

reme – children

Sabuknu – chief

sannu – saint

soto – want

wani – blind

udi – deaf

_____

la buti – I agree

ike buti – disagree

o la buti – agreed

o la – was, were

kili ike – why not?

Page from the Jesuit priest's mysterious word list.

14

The boy said, "Maybe true, father."

The father said nothing more.

Back in the son's room the explorer asked the boy his name.

"Carlito," he said with his trademark grin.

The explorer smiled. "A good name," he said. "Like my son's."

"His name Carlito too?" the boy asked, eyes widening.

"Charles," the explorer said. "They're the same. We used to call him Charlie. They probably still do," he said.

"He not come with you," the boy said.

"I think he's still in school," the explorer said.

"He still in school," the boy repeated.

The next morning the boy Carlito led the explorer (with the father's old manila envelope in hand) into the native district that ringed the little port city. They picked their way slowly through an endless network of alleys, past row upon row of makeshift shacks crackling with sounds of life. Native children crisscrossed the alleyways laughing and calling to each other. Here and there dark-skinned figures sat in doorways watching. But whenever the explorer tried to make eye contact, faces looked away. This was not going to be easy. But then one old native looked back when the explorer made a friendly gesture.

"Good day to you, uncle," the explorer said, coming up to him. "You are well?"

The old native gave no reply but did not seem put off by the approach of a white stranger. "Tell me, uncle," the explorer said, "will the good weather hold? What do you say?"

The old native said nothing and waited. White men do not come into back alleys to talk about weather.

"Uncle," the explorer went on, "I am told there may be *Chiroki* here. From the interior. Is that so, do you know?

The old man did not answer

"Will you tell me something else, good uncle," the explorer went on. "Some people say there is a strange tribe that lives up in the mountains, above the headwaters of the great river, beyond the *Chiroki*. They say these people make no sound when they talk. Do you know about them, uncle? Are there people like this back in those mountains?"

The native sitting in his doorway peered up at the explorer but did not answer. The explorer was about to give up when the boy Carlito spoke up in rapid-fire *patois*, pointing to the explorer. As the old native listened, a glint stole into his eyes and then abruptly he got up and walked off. The explorer, seeing opportunity, took off after him, Carlito right behind. The native led them through one alley after another until they came into a near-deserted lane at the ghetto's farthest edge. Most of the shacks lining the lane were empty, abandoned to rot and weeds, but the old man stopped in front of a tidy shack oddly unlike its neighbors. He pointed to its open doorway and then, just as abruptly, he turned and went off.

The shanty lacked a door and the explorer could see someone inside looking out. He approached the entrance, joined his hands before him and called out, "Hello, friend! Will you do me the honor? A few words with you?"

A tall, sturdy native suddenly filled the doorframe. He

was perhaps sixty years of age, with a bearing that said he was not to be fooled with. "Why you come?" he said. His voice was anything but inviting. The explorer noted his skin color had more bronze than the locals. And his *Moulawi* had a different ring. This was not a coastal native.

"Friend," the explorer said, "I am told you can help me. Can we talk?"

"What you want?" the native repeated, his presence blocking the doorway.

"I am looking for someone who knows *Chiroki*. The language," he said. "I am told you might be able help us."

The native regarded the white man, eyes moving up and down, and then over at the native boy by his side. "Why you want know?" he said finally. "Why you come?"

"If we can talk," the explorer said, "I will explain."

The lad, Carlito, impatient to be useful, leapt in with his stream of rapid-fire *patois*, nodding and grinning, using the word *Chiroki* and pointing to the manila folder in the explorer's hand. After a few moments of this, abruptly, the native backed inside and looked behind for the two to follow.

CHAPTER TWO

THE MYSTERY UNFOLDS

THE SHANTY WAS A SINGLE ROOM, no chairs, no furniture, but the dwelling had an orderly feeling and the floor mats were remarkably clean. Bare wall openings for windows let in plenty of light. They took positions on mats facing each other. The native waited for the white man to speak.

The explorer got right to the point. "I have come to your country to do research, to study language," he said. "I plan to go into the interior. To the *Chiroki.*"

The boy was about to launch into his own presentation, pointing to the manila envelope, when a look from the explorer cut him short. With a nod to the boy, the explorer opened the manila envelope and took out the single sheet with its cryptic one-line message, *Teeku: Tell Sabuknu I offer my death for them.*

"There's a word here," the explorer said, pointing to the page. "*Sabuknu.* We think it must be a *Chiroki* word. Do you know it's meaning?" he asked.

The native's eyes narrowed. "How you know that word?" he asked.

"There are a few of these words here I can't recognize," the explorer said waving the sheet. "It's a message written by a priest, many years ago," he said. "I believe he must have been with the *Chiroki*."

"And there's a name," the explorer quickly added, encouraged by the native's alert reaction. "*Teeku*. That must be a *Chiroki* name, no?" he said.

The native let out a visceral cry, leapt up and turned his back. Then he swung around, his face flushed. "That my name," he said. His black native eyes were piercing. "Where you get this?" he demanded.

"Priest give my father," the boy said, seizing his right to speak. (The explorer did not own the manila envelope yet. The father and son were working out a price.)

The native looked down at the boy. "When this happen?" he pressed.

"Priest give to grandfather," the boy said, correcting himself. "Grandfather give to father. Long time ago."

The native sat down, eyes fixed back on the explorer. "Why you come here?" he asked, calming. "What you want?"

"You know this priest!" the explorer said, barely able to conceal his excitement.

"I know priest," the native said.

"Damian?" the explorer said.

"*Katalan* Damian," the native said.

"Yes, *Katalan* Damian," the explorer said with a huge nod, tapping the paper.

"It mean priest," the native said.

The explorer's eyes were flaring with excitement. "This message was written to you," he cried, shaking his head, almost laughing at the coincidence.

"What message say?" the native demanded.

"Let me read it to you," the explorer said more

evenly. He knew it was not likely the aborigine could read. He held the paper up before him, pronouncing the words slowly and deliberately: *"Teeku,"* he read. *"Tell* Sabuknu *I offer my death for them."* Looking over at the native, he added, "Then there's his signature, *Katalan* Damian."

Teeku closed his eyes and went off to another place. The explorer remained silent and waited, but inside he was churning. He had not been in this country twenty-four hours and already he was sitting with a *Chiroki,* one no less who knew this mystery priest Damian. Lady Luck was outdoing herself!

Teeku opened his coal black eyes, his expression softer now. He looked at the explorer. "Let me see message," he said.

The explorer handed it to him. The aborigine studied the page, his head swaying almost imperceptibly. It was clear he could not read. After a few moments, looking up, he said, "I bring *Katalan* down river. Forty years ago."

Carlito jumped in, "Father say priest have bad animal wounds."

Teeku looked at the boy for a moment, then said to the explorer, "Mountain hyena attack *Katalan. Katalan* lose blood, know he maybe die. He want come coast. *Sabuknu* tell me bring him."

"Is *Sabuknu* the name for your chief?" the explorer asked.

Teeku nodded, "*Sabuknu* my father, *Maku,* son of *Timan.*"

Then you are *Teeku,* son of *Maku,*" the explorer said with a bright smile.

The aborigine just looked at him.

The boy jumped in, "Priest die in father's house."

Teeku turned to him. "*Teeku* see *Katalan* once in house. Maybe your house."

The boy's eyes widened. The explorer took the paper back and carefully replaced it in the manila envelope, winking at Carlito's glance of approval. Turning to *Teeku*, he said, "Tell me about this priest, *Katalan* Damian. Did he live with the *Chiroki* long?"

And thus begins a story that only deepened the puzzling mystery of this silent tribe. Struggling with the more formal *Moulawi*, *Teeku* tells the explorer that, many years ago, *Katalan* Damian came up river, all alone. Priest just show up one day in *Chiroki* territory, a pale, strange-looking intruder. *Chiroki* never see white man before. But *Katalan* not afraid and *Chiroki* see he carry good spirit and so they not kill him. Priest live with *Chiroki* and do many good things for *Chiroki* people and he become much loved. That make evil spirits angry. One day *Katalan* and *Teeku's* father, *Maku*, go up in mountains. Evil spirits enter hyena with plan to kill priest. Good spirit not let *Katalan* die, but animal make many bad wounds and *Katalan* lose much blood. *Katalan* say want go back coast. *Teeku* take priest down river and bring hospital. Doctors try but wounds infected bad and doctors say can do nothing. Then one day *Katalan* send for *Teeku*. *Teeku* find *Katalan* in bed in strange house. He dying now. *Katalan* only speak few words, tell *Teeku* go home, not stay on coast. *Teeku* make promise.

"*Teeku* not keep promise," he said simply. After a moment, he added, "River tribes kill *Chiroki*."

"But the river tribes let you come down," the explorer said.

"*Teeku* with priest," he said. "They not kill priest. They know *Katalan* have good spirit."

After absorbing this, the explorer said, "*Teeku*, now let me tell you why I am here, why it was so important for me to meet with you, a *Chiroki*. About two years ago, back home where I come from, I read a book by this priest, *Katalan* Damian. He wrote of certain strange rumors about an unknown tribe back in the mountains just beyond the hills where your people live, a tribe who speak and move without making a sound. It does not seem possible, but this priest intended to find out how such a thing could be, how a tribe could live and speak without making sound of any kind. And, frankly, that is why I am in this country now. And why I have come to talk to you. Can you tell me, my friend, are there mountain people like this beyond the hills of your villages, people who live and speak in total silence? You must know about them, if the story is true."

Teeku studied the explorer, his eyes hardening, but he said nothing.

"Do you know if *Katalan* Damian found this tribe?" the explorer pressed on.

Teeku did not answer, his eyes like onyx by now.

"I plan to go up the river, to your people," the explorer said. Peering into uninviting eyes he said, "Perhaps you can come with me." The explorer smiled and added, "Then you can keep your promise."

Teeku shook his head. After a moment, the native

said, "River tribes kill *Chiroki*." Then softening, he added, "Maybe kill you also."

"I am not afraid of that," the explorer said half smiling.

"I go too," Carlito chimed in with a grin. "I not afraid."

Teeku let out a little laugh. Looking hard at the explorer, he asked, "Why you want know about these people?"

"I am a scientist," the explorer said. "If there were such people, people wrapped in complete silence like that, the world would like to know about it." He paused and then added, "My guess is that this may be a religious commune of some kind, living with vows of silence. Something like that in this part of the world would be quite fascinating."

The explorer looked at *Teeku* hopefully. He could not be sure he was being understood. Then he said, more simply, "There are people like this living in the mountains above your villages, aren't there," he said more than asked.

Teeku hesitated for a long moment, and then nodded his head.

"Have you seen them?" the explorer asked, encouraged.

"No," *Teeku* said after a pause.

"Did *Katalan* Damian get to see them?" he asked.

Again *Teeku* hesitated. "No," he said finally.

"He never got to them?" the explorer persisted.

"No," *Teeku* said.

"What do your people say about them?" the explorer asked.

"No one speak about them," *Teeku* said. "It not good speak about them." He looked away at this.

"Can you tell me why?" the explorer persisted.

"Nobody speak about them," *Teeku* said, turning back.

The explorer tried again. "Tell me," he said, "did anyone ever tell you this tribe lives in silence?"

The aborigine considered the white man seated before him, and then finally he said. "They not speak."

"How do you know that?" the explorer asked.

"Father *Maku* say they not hear," *Teeku* said, looking down.

"They're deaf? the explorer exclaimed.

"They not hear," *Teeku* repeated.

"Did your father ever see them? Did he ever visit them?" the explorer asked.

"I not know," *Teeku* answered. Again he looked away.

"Do they come to your villages sometimes?" the explorer pressed on.

Teeku shook his head.

"Has anyone ever seen them?"

"They no come off mountain."

"Why?" the explorer insisted.

Teeku was silent for a long moment, considering his answer, then looking directly at the explorer and raising a hand to his eyes, he said, "They no see. They blind."

"They are all blind?" the explorer cried, resisting a laugh. "But that's not possible," he said.

"They blind," *Teeku* repeated.

The explorer leaned back and a troubled, ironic smile

stole across his face. But then that must be it after all, he reflected, what this is all about. Folklore. Simple native folklore. It's too absurd to be anything more. And he's been taken in by it. What else could it be? No one has ever seen them. He'd encountered tales as wild as this often enough in his expeditions, native stories told at night around campfires, of shadowy three-headed monsters that steal babies and so on. Tales in this case that made it to the coast as rumors. Even this priest Damian was taken in. A deaf and blind tribe living on a dark mountain, *sure, why not?* Probably they fly as well. That has to be all this is—the workings of over-stimulated primitive imaginations. Had he come half-way around the world for something so self-evident as this? Why hadn't he known better?

"You have been very helpful to me," the explorer said, moving to get up.

But in the next instant *Teeku* added something that set the explorer right back down. He said *Maku,* his father, was taking *Katalan* into the mountains to see these people when hyena attack.

"Really?" the explorer said, settling back. "Why were they going there?"

"*Katalan* go heal them," *Teeku* said.

"To heal them? Are you certain of that?"

"*Katalan* go heal them," *Teeku* repeated.

The explorer's eyes should have rolled at this. But something didn't make sense. Would this exquisitely educated Jesuit venture into untamed mountains to heal a campfire tale? That didn't figure. Something had to have motivated the priest to go up into those mountains, something more real than a fairytale. And what were those cryptic words this Jesuit scrawled out for *Teeku*. How did it go? *"Tell Sabuknu I offer my death for them."* Who was the priest referring to? Was the "them" this fabled mountain tribe? Could it really be they are blind too, both blind and deaf? And this priest was actually going there to try and heal them?

The explorer considered the native across from him. He was aborigine to the core—primitive, ignorant of the civilized world, head filled with who knows what fantasies. But still there was something in the way he held himself, the honest, simple way he spoke. A certain straightforwardness, a kind of nobility even.

"Was there some reason why you personally took *Katalan* down the river," the explorer asked. "You knew you could never go back."

"*Sabuknu* pick *Teeku*," the native said.

"Did the chief, your father, pick you because you . . . you offered yourself," the explorer asked.

"*Teeku* youngest son," the native said. Then, after a pause, he added, "Older brother, *Matsitu,* son of *Maku,* become chief when father die. Father pick *Teeku* because youngest son not necessary."

"I see," the explorer said.

A long, absorbing silence followed that no one seemed willing to break, not even young Carlito. Then finally the explorer spoke up. Looking at *Teeku*, he said, "Tell me about the river."

And with that, a long and perilous river journey was conceived and set in motion. The aborigine, *Teeku,* would help in unexpected ways while the boy, Carlito, saw visions of breakaway adventure with a new-found father from across the seas.

CHAPTER THREE

PREPARATIONS

THE EXPLORER, OF COURSE, talked to others in the coastal port about his plan. Everyone he spoke to said he was mad to consider such a thing. The river tribes were hostile, and the farther up you went, the more dangerous it became. Whites never venture upriver that far, they said, not even local traders. And no one has ever gone up to the headwaters, to the *Chiroki*. Yes, missionaries now and then have tried, but most never came back. As for these notorious mountains the explorer planned to enter, they are rumored to teem with huge poisonous snakes and even some sort of predatory bird. The natives themselves won't go up into those mountains. They think they're filled with devils. And besides, they protested, none of this nonsense about a deaf and blind tribe could possibly be true.

The explorer was a sensible man and was far from foolhardy about any of this, but nothing he heard could deter him. He'd faced unfriendly tribes before, in other expeditions. He knew how to handle himself. In his experience, unfriendly natives, even aborigines, strike out only if they feel threatened or have a grievance, or expect to gain something. They don't kill just for the pleasure of killing, not even game. Not normally. The important thing was not to provoke them. And if you offer them gifts, something bright or curious they had never seen before, and if you show that you are not afraid of them, you get along. It's always been that way. As for wild animals, he would have a gun. And all this talk about mountains infested with evil spirits only brought a tolerant smile to this clear-headed son of the Enlightenment. As for the rampant skepticism that none of this nonsense could possibly be true, the explorer's original intuition remained unshaken: something extraordinarily unusual was going on in those mountains and he would do well to find out about it. That was the priest Damian's belief and by now he shared it no less profoundly. Even if it should turn out to be nothing after all, the adventure would make an eminently publishable story.

So he set about preparing. There were many more meetings with *Teeku.* Initially wary, the aborigine little by little began to trust the white foreigner and in the end became no less invested in the project. Carlito for his part never left the explorer's side. And so over the next weeks, the project steadily advanced.

First the explorer had to understand the river. He would be on it for weeks, working against the current the entire way. Happily the river for the most part was wide and lazy. *Teeku,* in his broken formal *Moulawi,* said the explorer would encounter patches of white water now and then but if he kept to the banks he could manage without portage. This last piece of information came as great relief to the explorer. He liked Carlito well enough but he had no desire to bring along a second pair of hands, not even eager hands like this boy's.

Then there were the river tribes. *Teeku* warned the explorer he had to be very careful whenever he came into their presence. "Cross arms over chest and make low bow," *Teeku* said. "Bow show respect and arms across chest say you give no trouble. Maybe they not kill you," he said. Then there was the language problem. Each of the river tribes had its own language. Scouring the shops of the port city, the explorer filled a sack with colorful, beaded necklaces and shiny trinkets—a language all would understand.

But more than anything the explorer had to get a handle on the *Chiroki* language. He offered *Teeku* a small sum of money for his help, which the aborigine seemed pleased to accept. The explorer also purchased Christopher Damian's *Chiroki* word list from Carlito's father, meeting his stiff price. The word list was a natural place to start. (The explorer saw no reason to purchase the priest's cryptic message to *Teeku*.) And so for the next several weeks, with a voice recorder in hand, the explorer had *Teeku* pronounce the *Chiroki* words on Damian's list, words like *river, mountain, tribe, sound, silence, deaf, blind, father, son, daughter*, along with some other less likely words, like *curse, spell,* and *evil spirit*. With *Teeku* as informant, the explorer worked out the rudiments of *Chiroki* grammar and sentence structure and learned how to say simple things. All of this the explorer captured on his voice recorder and planned to replay over and over as he made his way on the river.

With help from Carlito, the explorer found a sturdy, native-built canoe and began outfitting it with gear for the journey—ponchos, rope, fishing tackle, knives, a pair of high-beam flashlights, strong binoculars and other such things useful for survival, or for barter in tight situations. He also took on board a quantity of medical and first-aid supplies. And, to be sure, a handgun and good supply of ammunition. He gave Carlito a small salary to watch over everything during the night hours, and every night thereafter the boy slept in the boat he expected would soon be taking him on the adventure of his life.

Not long after the native-built canoe was in the water, *Teeku* showed up at the dock. The sixty-year-old native leapt down into the canoe so deftly it barely rocked. He fingered the ribs and ran his hand along the hull skin, then he looked up and smiled. Back up on the dock, he warned the explorer that some parts of the river have flesh-eating fish. *Teeku* handed the explorer a small cloth bag filled with red powder. "If canoe turn over," *Teeku* said, "spread powder in water. Powder keep killer fish away." Then *Teeku* said, "When river narrow and current become more quick and you see mountains very close, you go careful." *Teeku* looked intently at the explorer. "*Chiroki* watch you come now."

"Are the *Chiroki* so hostile?" the explorer asked.

"Here river and hills belong *Chiroki*," *Teeku* said. "*Chiroki* not like stranger."

The explorer smiled. "They let the priest in," he said.

Teeku nodded. "Priest carry good spirit."

The explorer had to laugh. "I'll find a way," he said.

Teeku said nothing more. He hunched down on the dock, watching silently as the explorer busied with the boat, the ever-hovering Carlito lending a hand wherever he could. It struck the explorer that *Teeku* would never cease measuring him. The moment the explorer climbed back on the dock, *Teeku,* jumped up. "*Chiroki* have sign," he said, reaching out to touch him. *"Teeku* show." *Teeku* held up three fingers and then tapped his forehead and then three points across his chest. He did this three times, very slowly, with head lowered. "Only *Chiroki* know sign," *Teeku* said. "You make sign, *Chiroki* know you friend."

The explorer imitated the gesture, with three fingers first tapping his forehead and then three points on his chest. "Three times, you say?" he asked.

"Three times," *Teeku* answered. "Head down."

"Head down," the explorer said, half-jesting. "I'll remember that."

Teeku kept studying the explorer. He had the primitive's way of looking *into* a person before speaking his mind. After a while he said, *"Teeku* ask good spirit protect you."

The native's words drew a warm smile. The explorer had truly come to like this simple aborigine.

The day to shove off finally arrived. As the explorer took on last minute provisions, *Teeku* appeared on the dock. He stood there for a few minutes watching, saying nothing. But the tall, sturdy native had unfinished business.

"What is it, my old friend?" the explorer said.

Teeku took a small pouch made of snakeskin from around his neck.

"You give *Sabuknu*," he said, holding it up, making a reverent bow as he did so.

"What is it?" the explorer said.

"It belong *Katalan*. Tell *Sabuknu Katalan* want *Chiroki*

have. Tell *Sabuknu Teeku*, son of *Maku* give you. *Sabu-knu* now probably my oldest brother. He understand."

"OK, sure, I'll do that for you," the explorer said. He took the object and examined it. The small, snakeskin packet was indeed finely made. Inside he felt something metallic. "What's in it?" he asked.

"Odilia sannu," *Teeku* said, an unfamiliar note in his voice. The native took the packet back, bringing it to his lips, and then he tried to place the pouch around the explorer's neck. The explorer fended him off.

"What the devil is it?" the explorer asked.

In his halting formal *Moulawi*, *Teeku* tried to explain. He related that after they came down the river, he saw *Katalan* only one more time, just before he died. The priest was in this little room. He was alone and he was unconscious. But then suddenly he opened his eyes and saw *Teeku* standing by his bed. He motioned for *Teeku* to bend close to him. He was very weak but, even so, he rose up and, with much effort, he took *Odilia sannu* from around his neck and placed it over *Teeku's* head. It was something the priest always wore that way. After that, *Teeku* went on, *Katalan* sank back down and in a weak voice, he began to speak. He told *Teeku* he must go back up the river to his people and that he was to give *Odilia sannu* to *Sabuknu*, his father. *Odilia sannu* belong to *Chiroki* now, the priest said, his voice so unsteady *Teeku* could barely make out the words. But it was clear what the priest wanted. *Teeku* promised he would do these things, but he knew he was not telling the truth. He could never keep that promise. After *Katalan* spoke these things, the priest closed his eyes and maybe

The Chiroki *native,* Teeku *asks the explorer
to bring a magic object upriver to the*
Chiroki *tribal chief.*

he never opened them again. In any case, *Teeku* never saw him after that.

"*Teeku* not keep promise," he said, his dark, steady eyes holding the explorer. "But you go on river," he said. He held up the snakeskin packet. "Now you bring," he said, a radiant smile lighting his eyes. "For *Katalan*."

"I'll do it for *you*, my friend" the explorer said, only half-interested in what he was being told.

Teeku lifted the packet to his lips and again thought to place it over the explorer's head but backed off. Putting it in the explorer's hands, he said, "*Odilia sannu* have special power. *Odilia sannu* protect *Katalan* on river. Maybe now protect you."

"Not a bad idea," the explorer said with a laugh. He took the object and passed it over to Carlito to stow among his things. But it puzzled him. It was understandable that an aborigine would see magic powers in a talisman like this, but why a sophisticated Jesuit, why someone with all that learning? Why would the priest wear such a thing around his neck?

The explorer glanced at *Teeku*. "I've been meaning to ask you," he said. "About this priest. What sort of man was he? I've wondered about him."

Teeku hesitated, then said simply, "*Katalan* good man." Lowering his eyes, he added, "He special."

"So it seems," the explorer said, eyeing the native curiously. "But in what way exactly? Did he give your people gifts?"

Teeku looked up at the explorer but did not answer. He seemed unable to explain himself and the explorer, for his part, left it at that.

Finally the time to leave had come. Last minute provisions were brought aboard—flasks of water and tins of hardtack, jerky, nuts, dried fruit, a sack of flour, etc. Now everything was ready. It was a sad moment for Carlito whose father would not hear of his son traveling up the river. As it was, the explorer never intended to bring the boy and he was glad to be spared that unpleasant task of telling him. The explorer thanked the downcast lad for all his good help and then slipped him and *Teeku* each a handsome bowie hunting knife.

Then *Teeku* did an unexpected thing. The explorer had always noticed *Teeku* wore a heavy ring on his third finger of his right hand. *Teeku* now took the ring off his finger and gave it to the explorer.

"For my friend," he said.

The explorer took it but hesitated. "Is this from your people?" he asked.

"It family ring," *Teeku* said, then adding, "for men of family."

The explorer placed *Teeku's* ring on the third finger of his own right hand and thanked him warmly with a handshake. Happily it fit well. And that was that. The explorer climbed down into his canoe, looked up at his two friends a final time and pushed off.

As he moved away, *Teeku* called out from the dock with a final word. "Look for Lost Mountain," he cried. "That where hyena attack *Katalan*." He repeated the words, "Lost Mountain."

"How do you say Lost Mountain in *Chiroki*?" the explorer called back.

"*Dundi lano*," *Teeku* shouted.

"*Dundi lano,*" the explorer echoed as the canoe footed out into the river. Standing on the little pier, *Teeku* and Carlito watched him go, Carlito grinless, *Teeku* whispering *Chiroki* prayers, both lingering until the canoe passed from sight.

CHAPTER FOUR

CONFRONTATION ON THE RIVER

THE EXPLORER'S JOURNEY ON THE RIVER was uneventful for the first few weeks. The weather was pleasant and the lazy, contrary current posed no hardship. Each day he made good progress. The natives who dwelt along the river nearer the coast kept an eye on him but did not seem unfriendly. When he waved to them, once or twice some figure on the bank could be seen returning the signal. At night he would find a spot on the riverbank and build a little fire to cook fish he had caught. He was certain the natives knew he was there but the nights passed undisturbed. And in the morning he left a few colored trinkets by the campfire coals. Further up the river, though, the mood seemed to change. There was no waving back and the natives appeared to be watching him more intently.

Then suddenly one morning he found two longboats trailing him, keeping at a distance. Viewing them in his binoculars he saw no war paint, no sign of spears and figured most likely their purpose was to keep him from coming ashore in their district. At night they let him build a fire and camp undisturbed by the river edge, just yards from the water. But soon as morning arrived and he was back on the river, the longboats were there again off in the distance. The longboats followed him that way for several days until one morning one of them began drawing closer, narrowing the distance until barely a hundred yards separated them. Remembering what *Teeku* told him, the explorer swung his canoe about, then slowly crossed his hands over his chest and made a low bow. Good old *Teeku*, the peace gesture worked like he said it would! Almost at once, the longboat fell away. A day later the boats disappeared. The natives on this part of the river were leaving him alone. Or perhaps it was simply that he had passed beyond the territorial limit of this particular tribe.

All this time on the river the explorer practiced the *Chiroki* language, playing *Teeku's* voice recordings over and over. He grew adept at forming simple *Chiroki* sentences and asking simple questions. Certainly it wasn't much and problems would arise when the *Chiroki* spoke back with unfamiliar words. But he was a linguist and he would manage somehow.

He had been on the river a number of weeks and by now was deep into the interior. In the distance he could see mountains. Somewhere among them must be *dundi lano,* the Lost Mountain. Why did *Teeku* call out to him about *dundi lano*? Was *Teeku* clueing him where to find this silent, sightless tribe?

The mood along the banks had changed. Excited males could often be seen peering at him, running along the shore, shouting to each other and pointing. Yet nothing more happened. Once or twice he called out *loki loki* to them, hello in *Chiroki*, but got no response. Looking at them through his binoculars, he saw no sign of *Teeku's* bronze coloring. This was still not *Chiroki* country. At night, when he was ashore by the river's edge, he kept a strong fire going and slept very lightly, his gun at his side. But apart from the occasional sound of an animal or a bird cry coming from the thicket, the night hours passed quietly.

After another week on the river, the distant mountains drew close. The river had narrowed and stronger currents made the going more difficult. Strangely, no natives were now to be seen along the banks and the quiet struck the explorer as ominous. Very likely he was entering *Chiroki* territory, and if *Teeku* was right, things could shortly turn more perilous.

He did not have to wait long to find out. The very next morning, laboring his canoe around a river bend, there in the distance the explorer spotted a line of longboats coming downstream towards him. Grabbing his binoculars, he saw six boats, each filled with natives paddling furiously towards him, faces covered with war paint. Spears like porcupine quills festooned the boats. Moving with a fierce rhythm, the armada steadily narrowed the distance separating them. The explorer braced himself, reached for his hand gun, unlocked the safety and stuck the weapon in his belt. There were more of them than he could handle, but he would put up a good fight at least.

With the current in their favor, the on-coming armada bore down until they were barely fifty yards away. Then abruptly, at a signal from a figure in the lead boat, the flotilla stopped and the two sides lay there in the water, bronze-skinned warriors staring at the pale, strange-looking intruder. For long minutes nobody moved as the current began carrying them downriver. It struck the explorer that the *Chiroki* were satisfied to have him drift

A fleet of Chiroki *longboats descends upon the intruder.*

back down out of their territory. They did not plan on killing him so long as he did not cross their line.

The explorer set his paddle astride the canoe, folded his hands over his chest and made a low bow, exactly as *Teeku* had taught him. But the gesture had zero effect. In the next instant, at a signal from their leader, the native flotilla began back-paddling to arrest their downstream drift, increasing the separation between them. The explorer at once took up his paddle and started to work his way back upstream to them, but spears were leveled at him.

The explorer called out *loki, loki* (hello) and kept coming. These unexpected *Chiroki* words shouted across the water this way caused a stir. The natives peered at him and could be seen exchanging glances. But startling as this was, he was not to enter. As the explorer drew nearer, the leader gave a signal and a single spear was hurled at his canoe, perhaps by design only narrowly missing the hull's waterline and sinking him. The explorer set his paddle down and once again started drifting away with the current.

Then, mercifully, that special sign *Teeku* had taught him sprang to mind. Only *Chiroki* knew it, *Teeku* said. He wished he had paid the ritual more attention when *Teeku* showed it to him that time on the dock. Hoping he got it right, the explorer very deliberately held up three fingers out before him, then placing them on his forehead he tapped his brow slowly, and then again on three points of his chest, bowing his head as he did so. He remembered he was to repeat it three times, head down.

The effect was electric. Animated talk broke out at

once among the longboats. Before long someone laughed and others began stowing their spears. The lead longboat broke away and drew to within ten yards before it held off. The leader, a sturdy, well-built native, shouted something the explorer could not understand. The explorer called back, *chilani, chilani* the word for *friends.* (Repeating the noun twice makes it plural.) The leader answered back with something the explorer again could not grasp. And then silence. The explorer tried pulling closer to the longboat barely ten yards off but gave it up when he saw the leader stiffen. Laying his paddle down, he shouted as best he could in *Chiroki*, pointing to himself, "Friend of *Teeku*, son of *Maku*." The longboat leader looked stunned at this and the explorer nodded, bowed, and repeated the names, "*Teeku*, son of *Maku*." Then pointing back and forth to himself and to the longboat leader, he repeated over and over, "*chilani, chilani*."

The effect was startling. No doubt they all knew these names. To a man they turned to their leader to know what to make of it. But the longboat leader just stared at the intruder. He had no idea what he was supposed to do with this. The explorer for his part had started something but what could he do or say now, shouting this way across open water. The two kept peering at each other, the explorer searching for the right words, the longboat leader looking bewildered. He had been sent to keep the white intruder from entering their territory, but there were no instructions for anything like this. He again called out something the explorer could not get. "*Chilani* know only little-bit *Chiroki*," the explorer shouted back, underscoring the words with a gesture of futility. The longboat leader just stared.

Again his canoe began drifting away; something had to happen and happen fast. The explorer grabbed his paddle and pulled vigorously toward the longboats. Before they had a chance to react, he reached into his bag and took out one of his high-beam flashlights. Turing it on and holding it up for all to see, he played the beam of light back and forth along the water. The natives had never seen magic like this and became uneasy when the light spot edged too close to their boats. The explorer turned the spot on his own canoe and then onto his own body. "*Ladi, ladi,*" he shouted, *Chiroki* words for *OK* or *good* (repetition intensifies the adjective). Then, with the high beam pointing directly into his own face, the explorer held out the flashlight to the longboat leader. After some hesitation, the wary leader, eyes all fixed on him, motioned his men to pull closer. Drawing alongside, he reached over and took the flashlight, looked into the light and blinked, shook his head and laughed. He was not afraid. Then he began to shine it at the others. As the spot of light traveled among the boats, the explorer laughed and clapped his hands, shouting *ladi, ladi! (OK, good!).* Soon all the men were laughing. Who had ever seen anything like this? The longboats drew closer and the leader aimed the light into one face after another. Some threw up their hands and ducked, others clutched at the beam trying to catch it. Before long the military expedition dissolved into animated talk and merriment. The explorer, bringing his canoe alongside, leaned over and showed the leader how to turn the flashlight on and off. Then, pointing to the flashlight, he said, "*muti,*" *Chiroki* for *gift*.

There would be no better time than this. The explorer

bowed to the longboat leader and, pointing to himself, he said, "*Chilani (friend)* want see *Sabuknu*". At these words the longboat leader stared baffled at the explorer. "*Ladi?* (OK?) the explorer said, repeating the request. The leader continued to stare. This was beyond anything he was prepared to deal with.

The boats were drifting apart again. What more could be done? The explorer reached into his things and took out a handful of brightly colored, glass-bead necklaces. He held them up so that all the men could see. "Gift for *Sabuknu*," he said. He took one of the necklaces and held it out to the longboat leader by now already some yards away. "*Muti*," the explorer said, "*muti*." The native regarded the colored beads for a moment, then spun around and issued a brusque command to his men. The leader's longboat swung away, turned and began moving upstream, the others quickly falling in behind.

The explorer began at once to follow. Whenever the longboat leader looked back, the explorer would wave but no sign was sent in return. The explorer had difficulty keeping up with the flotilla and the distance separating them became worrisome. Then a strange thing happened. The native longboats stopped dead in the water and appeared to wait for him. Before he got too close they started up again but moved through the water more slowly now. Doubtless he had gotten to them because of the names. Here was a white-skinned intruder come up the river who knew the name *Maku*, the long-dead tribal chief. And *Teeku* son of *Maku*. They surely recognized the name of *Maku's* son, even after forty years.

After several hours the little fleet ahead of him drew

ashore. The explorer worked his way towards the landing where already a cluster of natives awaited him. The moment he touched the shore, men, women and children of all ages crowded down to his canoe, drinking in this curious, pale-skinned man off the river. He greeted them with a deep bow and ready smile, repeating *chilani* to each face before him, bringing reactions that were guarded but not in the least hostile. Word had already passed around that this odd-looking intruder was a kind of friend. Almost miraculously the explorer had managed a beachhead in this forbidden land.

The leader of the longboat flotilla came up and spoke evenly to the explorer. The explorer did not understand the words, but looking directly into the eyes of the leader and pointing to himself, told the leader, *"Chilani (friend)* want see *Matsitu* son of *Maku*, oldest brother of *Teeku."* At the mention of *Matsitu's* name the natives clustered around grew suddenly very still and turned to the leader to see what he would do. He did an unexpected thing. He stepped forward with the flashlight and tried to hand it back. The explorer shook his head. "No, keep," he said, *"muti (gift)."* Then on an impulse, the explorer reached into his canoe and took out his one remaining flashlight, holding it up for all to see. "This for *Sabuknu,"* he said clipping it on his belt. Then, pressing his luck, he said, *"Chilani* want go *dundi lano."* This mention of the Lost Mountain seemed to dumbfound the natives even more. Several became agitated and uttered things to the longboat leader that the explorer could not follow. At this, the longboat leader gave the explorer a strange look, turned on his heels and took off, disappearing into the bush. The explorer reached into his canoe, grabbed his gun and a backpack and took off into the bush after him, a long file of native warriors on the explorer's heels.

CHAPTER FIVE

AMONG THE *CHIROKI*

T HE SINGLE FILE TRAVELED THIS WAY uphill through the bush for several hours, the longboat leader moving at a brisk pace twenty yards in front, the explorer straining to keep up behind, and after him a line of war-painted males with spears. The natives moved through the undergrowth like antelopes, without a rustle. Finally they emerged into a huge, sunlit clearing dotted with a great number of dwellings. They were entering a *Chiroki* village of well-constructed, thatched-roofed huts arranged in orderly rows, many with small, neatly tended gardens around them. As this fleet-footed procession made its way past these huts, native women and children spilled out to watch them, some tagging along, shouting to others and stirring excitement as they went. The procession came to a halt in front of a large, ornate wooden structure in the center of the village. The longboat leader clapped his hands in a ceremonial way and at this signal everyone fell silent, waiting, eyes fastened on the entrance. Long moments later, there emerged from the dwelling an elderly man, borne on each arm by two men. He was adorned with multiple necklaces made of what appeared to be tiger's teeth. The explorer knew he was looking at *Sabuknu,* the tribal chief, and mostly likely at *Matsitu, Teeku's* older brother.

The longboat leader went up to *Sabuknu* and they touched each other's shoulder ceremoniously. The explorer heard the chief call the longboat leader *hindo*, *Chiroki* for *son*. As they spoke, the tribal chief glanced over at the explorer. Leaning heavily on his attendants, the old chief seemed irritated at the interruption of what may have been an afternoon siesta. But that changed the moment the longboat leader uttered the name *Teeku,* pointing at the explorer. The old tribal leader pushed himself away and peered long and hard at the pale-skinned intruder. The explorer crossed his hands across his chest and bowed but the gesture seemed to have little effect.

The longboat leader showed *Sabuknu* the flashlight he had been given but did not turn it on. They spoke together this way for several minutes, the old chief at most exhibiting annoyed interest. But when the words *dundi lano* were uttered, the chief bent forward and again squinted intently at the intruder standing there in the hot, mid-afternoon sun. In the next instant, the chief motioned that he wished to be led back inside with the longboat leader to join him. The explorer was kept where he stood, encircled by the longboat warriors in their war grease and the curious scrutiny of villagers.

The longboat leader came out moments later and beckoned the explorer to approach. In simple *Chiroki* he said *Sabuknu* would see him. The longboat leader led him into the dwelling, first through an antechamber where two attendants appeared to be standing guard, and then into a large, ornately painted room. The room was bare except for a small army of life-sized, brightly colored totems arrayed along the walls. At the far end *Sabuknu* sat alone, seated on a luxurious mound of leopard skins. Arranged on the floor around *Sabuknu* was a semi-circle of neatly crafted reed mats. As the explorer approached, still carrying his gun and backpack, *Sabuknu* gestured him to sit. The longboat leader took up a position by *Sabuknu* but remained standing.

No one spoke. The explorer waited for *Sabuknu* to break the silence but the tribal chief was in no hurry. The chief's eyes were expressionless, coldly measuring the white-skinned alien before him. The silence dragged on this way for some time. The explorer kept his eyes lowered, looking up only now and then with what he wanted to be taken as fearless respect. Then, finally, *Sabuknu* broke the silence with a gruff demand, "Why want go *dundi lano?*" The explorer, smiling, leaned forward and in halting *Chiroki* launched into a speech he had rehearsed many times on the river. He said he was honored to be in the presence of *Sabuknu*. He explained that he came in peace from the coastland, that he had learned about the *Chiroki* from *Teeku* son of *Maku*, who was his good friend. He said that *Teeku* son of *Maku* had told him good things about his people and taught him some words of the beautiful *Chiroki* language. Then the explorer stopped. The mention again of *Teeku* and *Maku* clearly stirred the old chief. There could be little doubt *Sabuknu* was *Teeku's* much older brother, *Matsitu*. The dark keenness in the eyes despite their age, the chiseling of the mouth, the broad, noble bronze forehead, all spoke of common stock.

Then the explorer held out his right hand bearing the heavy ring *Teeku* had given him. It was indeed a family ring, just as *Teeku* said. Both *Sabuknu* and his son wore rings of identical kind. "Ring gift from *Teeku*," he said in *Chiroki*, holding up his hand.

The chief was plainly intrigued, but wary. Here was this white-skinned intruder from the far distant coast come unaccountably into their midst, speaking their language, badly didn't matter, and above all claiming to know *Teeku*, the chief's long unseen younger brother whose very ring he wore. The explorer knew he had won the chief's attention. Now he had to gain his support. He wondered how this austere native chieftain would react to the use of his name, *Matsitu*. *Teeku* had told him to be careful with names. He said the *Chiroki* do not like strangers to have their name for fear it be used to harm them. And the explorer knew this from his other explorations. Primitives protect their names because a man's name gives access to his inner person. Names are the arrows of spells and incantations. But names also form the flowerbed of intimacy and friendship. *Teeku* said the *Chiroki* prefer names or titles to pronouns when they refer to each other and even when they refer to themselves. For instance, rather than using the *Chiroki* pronoun *no* to express the first person *I*, it was more customary to say *chilani-no* (*I-friend*) or even at times just *chilani* if the self-reference was clear. And you did not use the second person pronoun *nu (you)* when addressing someone, especially someone you respected. For persons of stature, you used their title, like *Sabuknu*. *Teeku* also told him if you address someone by that person's name, by his personal name, that meant there is a bond between you and him. It was worth a try.

The explorer leaned forward and explained that *Teeku* often spoke about his older brother. Keeping his eyes down, the explorer uttered the name *Matsitu*, son of *Maku*. But the gambit backfired. *Sabuknu* threw an angry glance at his son. Familiarity like this was an offense. Glaring fiercely now at the explorer, the chief stuck out an imperious finger and demanded, "Tell *Sabuknu* why want go *dundi lano!*"

The explorer bowed low and took a deep breath. Referring to himself as *chilani-no*, and at other times as *chilani-no na Chiroki* (*I-friend of the Chiroki*), he explained he had come up the river to meet *Sabuknu* and ask for the good chief's help. He intended to go to *dundi lano* and make contact with the tribe that lives on that mountain, the tribe that *Teeku* son of *Maku* told him about, the tribe that speaks without sound and that is also blind.

The explorer got no further. *Sabuknu* exchanged bewildered glances with the longboat leader, then both turned to the explorer, their eyes agape. *Teeku* had warned that the *Chiroki* do not talk about this mountain tribe, but he never explained why. Clearly the explorer had just violated a deep tribal taboo and the meeting was about to come to a bad end. He had to think of something fast. He fingered the flashlight on his belt. It had worked before on the river. He held it up for the chief to see. "Gift for *Sabuknu*," he said with a reassuring nod to the longboat leader who was still holding onto his. The explorer turned it on and played the light spot along the floor and on himself, and then, turning it off, held it out to the longboat leader to bring to his father. But the gesture only annoyed the chief. *Sabuknu* barked an order and instantly the longboat leader sprang forward and stood over the explorer, pointing to the door. Magic or no magic, the interview was over.

The longboat leader led him hurriedly through the village to a dilapidated hut at the edge of the clearing. "Stay here," he said firmly. "Tomorrow go river."

"No," the explorer said, trying to affect a friendly smile. *"Chilani-no na Chiroki mino dundi lano (I-friend of Chiroki go dundi lano)".*

The longboat leader's face hardened. "Not go *dundi lano*," he said, jaw thrust out. "Not go," he repeated. And with that the longboat leader smashed the flashlight down at the explorer's feet and took off.

It was late afternoon by now and before long the sun would be setting and it would be dark. He had been left without food or water. There was not even a mat on the damp earthen floor. Looking out an opening in the wall he could see two males nearby standing watch. He had no thought of giving up. He had come too far. Early in the morning he could try to evade the guards somehow and set out on his own. Yes, but how far would he get? And what would become of his canoe? It all seemed hopeless. Tomorrow they would take him down to the river and the current would carry him back to the coast, empty-handed, lucky perhaps to have escaped with his life. Things had been moving along so well and then this stone wall. Why? What was it about this Lost Mountain, this *dundi lano* and its mystifying tribe? One could almost believe those dark tales about this mountain. But whatever the story was, it looked like he would never get to tell it.

That night a sudden, violent electric storm arose seemingly bent on terrorizing the village. Already sleepless anyway, the explorer leapt up as thunder and lightning began crashing all around him, shaking and flooding the hut with explosions of light. Outside he heard the frightful sound of trees being split. A mighty, fierce wind rose and whipped the village with lashing rain. Water began seeping down through the rotting, overhead thatching and swept in through the wall openings. The explorer spent the next miserable hours protecting himself, his gun, ammunition and backpack from a drenching unlike any he had ever experienced.

For some reason, at the height of the storm, the explorer remembered that odd little object *Teeku* had given him at the dockside, the little snakeskin packet *Teeku* said the priest Damian wore around his neck. *Odilia sannu, Teeku* called it. The explorer never thought to ask what these words meant. What made him think of it just then was the unpleasant thought of seeing *Teeku* again not having done the favor asked of him. Just before he died, the priest had made *Teeku* promise to bring it to *Sabuknu*.

"Now you bring," *Teeku* had said to the explorer.

It would be a little miracle if he had it with him now. The explorer fetched his flashlight and rummaged through the backpack and, behold, there it was, the finely made snakeskin pouch, not even wet. Turning his back to the sheets of rain sweeping in through the wall openings and hunching his shoulders over the pouch, he opened it and let the metallic object inside slip out into his hand. Wedging the flashlight between his knees he rotated the object in its light and saw what looked like a tiny reliquary. The casing was of hammered gold with filigreed edging and glass face. It looked quite lovely and doubtless had come from the priest's part of the world.

The reliquary's glass face was smudged over. The explorer dipped his thumb in rainwater puddled about him and polished the glass. Peering with his flashlight, he saw a tiny, ivory-colored chip about the size of a grain of rice, and below it, on a little strip of paper, the words *S. Odilia*. The explorer knew quite well what he was looking at: the relic of a saint by the name of *Odilia*. And the tiny, brownish ivory chip had to be a bone fragment of the saint. The explorer had no idea who this *Odilia* may have been or why she (probably a *she*) was venerated as a saint. Or why this priest Christopher Damian wore the relic around his neck, and why, just before he died, he wanted *Sabuknu* to have it. Regrettably, he would never have answers to any of this. He had made his way to the center of a strange, exotic world riddled with mysteries that grew deeper by the hour, to be thrown out before getting to the bottom of a single one of them.

Outside, thunder and lightening kept terrorizing the village, wind and rain lashing the dwellings in angry blows. But storms don't last and in the morning, at first light, the explorer planned to do exactly what *Teeku* asked—he would bring this *Odilia sannu* thing to *Sabuknu*. He could never face *Teeku* again otherwise. And who knows, maybe *Teeku* was right and this thing might still bring him good luck. Strange, unexpected things have happened ever since he stepped off the freighter, beginning with Carlito and his father, and then *Teeku*. Weary now, with that faint glimmer of hope, the explorer fell asleep, holding the bone of a saint in his hand.

CHAPTER SIX

AN UNFORESEEN DEVELOPMENT

A T FIRST LIGHT THE EXPLORER emerged from his hut. The sky was clear and a rosy tinge in the eastern sky held promise of fair weather. He looked around for his native guards but none were in sight; the way was clear. He set out toward the center of the village. Downed branches were strewn everywhere, and here and there he had to wade ankle-deep through ponds of rainwater. He had not gone very far before native males began to fall in behind him, a few of them with spears. They did not try to stop him and in fact kept at what seemed like a purposeful distance. Maybe the storm had spooked them out. Maybe it was this pale-faced intruder who brought the night of terror down on them. On an impulse, he hung the snakeskin locket around his neck, the way *Teeku* said the priest had worn it.

Before long the entire village was awake. Women and children began appearing in doorways, uneasy eyes following this early dawn procession. As he neared *Sabuknu's* dwelling, a knot of native men were already there blocking the entrance, among them the longboat leader. They seemed uneasy. As the explorer approached, the longboat leader stepped forward and held up his hand—the explorer was to come no closer.

"Go away," he called out. The command was firm but the contempt of the previous day was gone.

"For *Sabuknu*," the explorer called back, holding up the little snakeskin pouch around his neck.

"*Sabuknu* not see," the longboat leader shouted.

The explorer drew nearer and native men began to press around him. He held out the snakeskin pouch hanging around his neck. "For *Sabuknu*," he repeated. Then the explorer made that special sign *Teeku* had taught him, slowly touching his forehead and three points across the chest, head held low. He did this three times. The ritual once again had its effect and the natives drew back.

The explorer again held out the snakeskin packet. "For *Sabuknu*," he said again. "From *Teeku*, son of *Maku*." He was at a loss to say more.

The longboat leader would not look at it. He said something to the men and in the next moment two of them took hold of the explorer by the arm.

"Go," the longboat leader said, his voice harder now. "You go away now," he said. Then he turned his back to the explorer.

The natives sought to draw the intruder away but he managed to break free. He had to deliver this thing around his neck. "*Odilia sannu!*" he called out, holding up the snakeskin packet, hoping the words would mean something. "*Odilia sannu!*" he shouted again, adding, "From *Katalan*."

The longboat leader froze. Slowly, as if transfixed, he turned around and scrutinized the explorer and the object in his hand. Then abruptly he disappeared inside.

Moments later the explorer was invited into the chief's dwelling. *Sabuknu* was already on his feet to meet him, the longboat leader beside him, both staring at the explorer with dazed, bewildered looks.

The chief made a gesture for the explorer to be seated, and took his own place on his seat of skins. This time the explorer did not wait for the chief to speak.

He held up the snakeskin pouch. "For *Sabuknu*," he said. "*Odilia sannu*, from *Teeku,* son of *Maku*," then adding, "from *Katalan*." The explorer removed the pouch from around his neck and leaning forward held it out. Neither native moved. The explorer rose, slipped the relic out from its pouch and set it on the mat a few feet from the royal seat.

"*Katalan* want *Sabuknu* have," he said. The explorer bowed and returned to his place on the mat.

The chief began speaking to the longboat leader who kept nodding at his words. The talk was animated and the explorer heard them utter *Teeku's* name, and *Katalan*, the word for priest. As they spoke, the old tribal chief repeatedly looked over at the explorer, his aged, dark black eyes lit up with astonishment. Finally his gaze fixed on the little object lying just before him on the mat. With effort, the old tribal chieftain got up and leaned over the relic. He bent down to get a closer look, and finally dropped to his hands and knees and thrust his face to within inches of the object. Then he sat back and gazed at the explorer—the long, penetrating look of an aborigine seemingly beyond time. The explorer lowered his head and waited.

Reaching for a hand from his son, *Sabuknu* got on his feet and returned to his seat of skins. He closed his eyes and remained that way, motionless, for many long minutes. When he opened them, the black eyes of this ancient aborigine were suffused with unfamiliar warmth.

As if suddenly reminded of his presence, the tribal chief looked over at the explorer, made a deep bow and turned to his son. They spoke together and again the explorer heard the word *Katalan*. After a short while the conversation ended and the chief turned back to the explorer and bowed. In the next instant the longboat leader was on his feet. He too bowed and gestured for the explorer to follow him outside. He led the explorer to a structure a few doors down on the village square and with a few simple *Chiroki* words invited him to remain there. The dwelling was well-built, clean and orderly, its dirt floor covered with fresh floor mats, suggesting the place was a tribal guest house. Satisfied that the explorer was comfortable, the longboat leader bowed and departed. Shortly, native women arrived carrying grains and fruits and a gourd of fresh milk. The explorer tried out a few *Chiroki* sentences on them, causing not a little merriment.

Unaccountably, for whatever reason, everything had changed. In the twinkling of an eye the bone chip of a saint had transformed him from outcast to honored guest. How this could be was beyond him. But whatever lay behind this change of fortune, the explorer felt recharged.

By now utterly famished, he took food, and after refreshing himself he stepped outside. Sunlight sparkled in the freshly scrubbed air as pools of rainwater shrank back into the earth. Guards were nowhere to be seen.

He was free to walk about. But *Sabuknu* clearly had something in mind and the explorer would stay right where he was.

He would not have to wait long. Several native women arrived with cakes and clay cups filled with warm herbal tea, and immediately behind came the longboat leader. He made a deep bow and seated himself. The two sat there sipping tea without speaking, barely making eye contact. But something was at work inside this native warrior and when it came out it left the explorer literally stunned.

The longboat leader looked up and again made a little bow. "*Katalan-nu,*" he began, addressing the explorer as honored priest (the *nu* suffix indicating high respect, as in *Sabuknu*). Then, pointing to himself, he said his name was *Teeku-mi* son of *Matsitu* (the *mi* suffix means *little*). He was named after his uncle *Teeku* son of *Maku*. *Sabuknu Maku* honored him with his uncle's name when he was still an infant, after *Teeku* son of *Maku* went down river with *Katalan-nu-lina (first honored priest)*. *Sabuknu Maku* gave him *Teeku's* name so that *Teeku* would be remembered. And now *Sabuknu Matsitu* is very pleased his younger brother *Teeku* has sent them a new *Katalan*. And most of all, *Sabuknu Matsitu* is honored with the gift of the saint.

The native's words left the explorer dumbstruck. They were taking him for a priest! A second *katalan* Damian. What in the world was he to do with that? And then, remarkably, this aborigine warrior had revealed his own name, along with his father's, *Matsitu*. This was no small thing. It meant they had accepted him as an intimate, all because they took him for a priest, come in the footsteps of that mysterious first priest. What had Christopher Damian done forty years ago to fling these doors wide open now, just because they took him too for a priest? He would shortly find out.

Teeku-mi, the longboat leader, again bowed and turned more solemn. *"Katalan-nu"* he said, *"Teeku-mi miso (take) Katalan dundi lano. Buti la? (Do you agree?)."*

The explorer could not bring himself to answer. Yes, wonderful, great, they were going to take him to *dundi lano,* the gate stood open, miraculously. But why the change of heart? What were they expecting him to do? He would go there as a scientist, never as a priest in some Jesuit's footsteps.

Not getting a response, *Teeku-mi* bent forward and again pointing to himself said slowly and more insistently, *"Katalan-nu, Teeku-mi miso (take) Katalan Jakareme."* (*Teeku-mi* will take priest to the *Jakareme.*)

Jakareme! The term was not new. He had seen it on Christopher Damian's list, along with its stark definition, *children of the curse.* The explorer never made the connection, but there it was. The *Jakareme* were the deafblind on *dundi lano* and the *Chiroki* looked upon them as cursed. This was why no one ever spoke of them. And why the priest Damian was on his way to the *Jakareme* when he was attacked. To heal them, *Teeku* said. Or did the priest have in mind to *uncurse* them (whatever that could possibly mean)? And now, unbelievably, in a short while he would be on *dundi lano* himself, mixing with this mysterious tribe. He had traveled halfway around the world and up a dangerous river, pursuing a fascinating scientific puzzle, and against all odds he was on the verge of solving it. But he was a man of science, not a priest. What were the *Chiroki* expecting him to do with these *Jakareme*?

The longboat leader stared at *Katalan* across from him. *"Buti la?"* he repeated, *"Buti la?"*

The explorer managed to nod and utter the words *"La buti" (Yes, I agree)*. Then, realizing his words had been flat and lifeless, he half-extended his hands the way he had seen a priest do. What choice did he have?

At this the longboat leader leapt up, made a profound bow and immediately withdrew, excitement spreading across his face.

The explorer sat there utterly confused. Everything had flipped about in his favor. He was being taken to the Lost Mountain all because of this crazy relic, this *Odilia sannu*. He had not paid the thing any attention, never asked *Teeku* about it, why it was thought so special. How weird this was. He happened to wear it around his neck and so to them he was a priest. It brought him their trust, even their affection because of it. And it would bring him to *dundi lano*. But as a priest, and he was no priest. The thought left him dazed.

Such thoughts came to a halt when of a sudden the air outside exploded with the pounding of drums. Many drums at first and then a single, persistent drum, telling of a message being sent, over and over. Soon the countryside was filled with the echo of drums relaying the message across the hills and the beat of distant drums in answer. In the midst of this eruption, *Teeku-mi* returned, his bearing serious but his eyes were burning with excitement. The chief's son made a low bow, sat down and immediately began to speak.

CHAPTER SEVEN

THE *CHIROKI'S* DREADFUL SECRET

T HE NATIVE PRINCE started out with what sounded like a litany of names, some familiar to the explorer, like *Timan*, *Maku*, *Matsitu*, others strange. The explorer grasped that, for some reason, the native was going over his genealogy. That gave the explorer an idea. He rolled up a floor mat and drew a stick figure in the dirt. "*Timan*," he said in *Chiroki*, pointing to the figure, "father of *Maku*." Then below *Timan* he drew another stick figure, "*Maku*, your grandfather," he said. Then beneath *Maku* he drew two stick figures side by side. "*Matsitu* and *Teeku*," he said, looking at up the native. *Teeku-mi* gave a nod and then himself bent over and drew a stick figure directly beneath *Matsitu*. "*Teeku-mi*," he said, pointing to his chest. Then the native drew another, smaller stick figure directly beneath the one for himself. "*Lunas-nili*," he said.

Timan
↓
Maku
↓
Matsitu Teeku
↓
Teeku-mi
↓
Lunas-nili

The explorer asked, "*Lunas-nili la hindo na Teeku-mi?*" (*Lunas-nili is son of Teeku-mi?*).

Teeku-mi shook his head. "*Lunas-nili la dochi*" (*Lunas-nili is daughter*), he said. At this a shadow fell across the warrior's face. He looked away and fell silent.

"*Chilani-no ike banyo*" *(I-friend don't understand),* the explorer said, breaking the silence.

The native looked back and nodded. Leaning forward, in what came to be an afternoon-long struggle with dirt drawings and half-understood words, all against the ceaseless background staccato of drums, this stalwart heir to the tribal throne unburdened his heart of a story no outsider would ever be allowed to hear. But this was different. The pale figure seated opposite him was a second *Katalan.* Like the first, he had miraculously come up the river to his people, carrying the magic saint.

What the explorer pieced together from all that was told him that afternoon is recorded below. The telling took much effort between the two, but by the time it was over, the explorer finally understood what it was he had blundered into.

Many, many generations ago (how many it was impossible for the explorer to learn), the *Sabuknu* of that long ago time was *Lominat.* *Lominat* had a grown son named *Kinusat.* An evil spirit from *dundi lano* came and inhabited *Kinusat* and brought him to rebel against his father. In the power struggle, *Kinusat* killed his father. *Kinusat* then became *Sabuknu.* Soon after, *Kinusat* had a son who was born deaf and blind. And then, after that, among the villages, every now and then other children were born who could not hear their mother's voice nor see the light of day. This is happening even to this day. The *Chiroki* see all this as signs that the spirits of *dundi lano* have placed an evil spell on them. That is why infants born this way are called *Jakareme (children of the curse).* The witch doctors and medicine men of the tribe are powerless against this spell. They say a *Jakareme* child must be taken to *dundi lano* and left there to appease the mountain gods. This was done from the beginning, and it has always been so, even now to this day. Some *Jakareme* are known to have survived on the mountain, kept alive by the spirits there to work their evil. So now somewhere on that mountain there are living *Jakareme*. No one knows how many but the *Chiroki* know for certain they are there.

Given the language barrier, the back and forth effort between them took up most of the afternoon. But *Teeku-mi* was not finished. Kneeling on the floor, he reached out to the stick figure of his daughter, *Lunas-nili*, and, looking to making sure *Katalan* was following, slowly traced a circle around his daughter's image. Peering up at *Katalan* he cried, *Jakareme!* Then, eyes clouding over, he sat back and looked away.

"Your daughter was left on *dundi lano?*" the explorer asked bluntly.

Teeku-mi looked back at the explorer but said nothing. The look in his eyes said enough. Then, abruptly, his expression lit up. Pointing to the stick figure for himself, he leaned over and drew a similar circle around his own stick image. *"Teeku-mi hoda o la Jakareme!"* (I too was a child of the curse!), he cried peering up at the explorer, eyes aflame. *"Teeku-mi hoda o la udi ka wani"* (I too was deaf and blind), he said, a strange smile stealing across his face. The aborigine sank back and stared at the explorer. Then again he reached down and drew a stick figure alongside his own. *"Katalan-nu-lina"* (first Katalan-nu), he said looking up. He traced a tiny line across the neck of the priest figure and said, *"Odilia sannu."* He glanced up to make sure *Katalan* was following, then he extended the line from *Odilia sannu* to the *Jakareme* circle around the figure for himself. And then, with a brusque gesture, he wiped the circle away. The native leaned back and said, *"Odilia sannu o galiva Teeku-mi"* (*Odilia sannu healed me*). The aborigine bowed and fell silent, his luminous eyes riveted on the *Katalan* across from him.

The explorer was at a loss. What *Teeku-mi* related was clear enough. The priest Christopher Damian had somehow cured him. Or so these aborigines believed. No wonder they revered a priest. But, come on, was such a thing even possible? And these natives traced the action back to this crazy relic he had unthinkingly worn around his neck like the Jesuit. Now he too was a priest, and they were expecting him to pick up where Christopher Damian left off. The priest was on his way to heal them when he was attacked by that animal! It couldn't be clearer. They had been taking the first *katalan* to *dundi lano* so that he could work more miracles! And now it was his turn. This aborigine prince was waiting for him to say, sure, I'll go up there and cure your daughter— what's her name—*Lunas-nili.*

A long silence fell between them and *Teeku-mi* began to stir uneasily. But what could the explorer say? That he was not a priest? That he did not believe in miracles? That if they took him to *dundi lano* he would do no such thing. That he was not a magician. All he wanted was to look around and gather what data he could about their number, the arrangement of their communal life, such as it was, and most importantly for him, how a band of deafblind like this managed to communicate with each other, and for that matter ever manage to hold onto life. For a second time in less than 24 hours his fabulous, once-in-a-lifetime adventure in science seemed doomed, this time for an unbelievably insane reason. The uneasy silence grew heavy, the native waiting, watching him, the explorer unable so much as to meet his gaze. He had never in his life ever felt so undone. The Jesuit Damian had gotten himself mauled, but for the priest it was only his body that suffered.

Then the drumming outside abruptly ceased, and as if on cue *Teeku-mi* leapt up and departed, this time not bothering to bow or even glance at the explorer. Without the drums, an eerie stillness descended over the village, as if the aboriginal world were holding its breath. The effort to follow the story had taken hours and the sun by now had long gone down. The explorer was left alone in the gathering darkness but it was not to be much longer. Suddenly, three native males dressed in ceremonial robes entered, each making a low bow. Two of them carried torches and the third, an elderly man, bore a white garment over his arm. The elder approached, bowing again, and held the garment out before him. The explorer saw at once it was a priest's liturgical vestment, a white alb, something the Jesuit Damian must have left behind. The elder, again bowing, approached to assist with the vesting, perhaps in just the way he had done forty years earlier, vesting a real priest for a liturgical ceremony. Who knows, perhaps even for a Catholic Mass. The explorer, swallowing hard, bent over to allow the white garment to be slipped over his head, watching it drape down to his feet. The elder handed him the cincture and the explorer tied it himself.

And with that act the explorer stepped into a priestly world, a world he knew nothing about and had no right to enter. But given the circumstances, this man of science had little choice. And so the fatal step was taken, wherever it might lead.

The two torch bearers and the elder then went to the door and swung it wide open. Outside a score of natives had already formed in a line, many bearing torches. Others were dressed in colorful, native ceremonial robes. At the head was a young male carrying a pole with a crucifix, doubtless something else the Jesuit had left behind. At the sight of the explorer vested now in an alb, a single drum began to tap, slowly, rhythmically. The elder led their new *Katalan* to the rear as the procession began to move.

The line halted in front of *Sabuknu's* dwelling where the native chieftain was already outside, leaning on the arms of two young native males. Beside him stood his son, *Teeku-mi*. Both father and son were garbed in elaborate ceremonial robes of many colors befitting their station in the tribe. To the explorer's increasing dismay, if that were possible, he saw *Teeku-mi* holding a liturgical chasuble, the finely made outer vestment traditionally worn over the priest's alb. *Teeku-mi* approached, made a profound bow. Averting the explorer's eyes, he slipped it over *Katalan's* head. Then *Sabuknu* hobbled forward. Supported by his attendants, he too made a profound bow and with a display of great reverence, took out from his robe *Odilia sannu*. Coming right up to this second *Katalan*, he placed the relic ceremoniously around the new priest's neck. Again bowing, *Sabuknu* and his son joined the procession just in front of the distraught explorer, and the line moved on, the natives intoning a low chant in company with the lone drum as it made its slow, deliberate way.

The procession entered a large field at the far edge of the village. It was night by now and torches were burning everywhere, playing off dark swaying figures stretching far out into the glowing darkness. As the procession entered, drums from the torch-lit darkness picked up the same low, steady rhythmic beat.

At the near end of the field rose a large, earthen mound. Arranged along its back stood a string of totems that had been moved for the occasion from *Sabuknu's* dwelling. These were interlaced with large, as yet unlit torches. In the center of the mound a table-like structure was set up to serve as altar. Back from the altar were placed three royal chairs. *Sabuknu*, his son *Teeku-mi*, and the explorer, *Katalan*, were each escorted up the mound and led to these positions. *Katalan* was shown to the center seat of honor. The torches at the back and side of the altar mound were then ceremoniously lit and the elevation became a blaze of light. And with that a low chant began wafting out from the vast shadowy presence in the torchlight-studded night. The explorer could not understand anything of the chant except for three words that sounded like the Latin phrase, *Ave Verum Corpus*. The words were repeated over and over. Perhaps he was mistaken but probably not; the Jesuit Christopher Damian had not wasted his time when he was here. If he actually healed *Teeku-mi*, a *Jakareme*, as the chief's son claimed, the tribe would inevitably look upon the priest as some kind of god. And now here he was, on stage before a field crammed with dark, swaying primitives, expecting who knows what as they peered at him, a man who had no religion, robed as a priest before an altar he would have to approach in very short order. What was he supposed to do? It was no wonder the explorer had trouble finding his breath.

Sabuknu stood up, bowed to the second *Katalan*, and then without assistance hobbled to the front of the altar mound and raised his two hands high above his head. The assembly fell silent. He began to speak, his strong voice carrying out into the night air. As his chieftain father spoke, the son stole glances over at the explorer. He for his part sat there, eyes lowered, concealing quiet desperation.

Sabuknu went on and on. The explorer, struggling with panic, barely listened. But at one point he saw the chief turn and point to his son. He heard the word *Jakareme,* and felt the darkness stir at this pronounce- ment. Then the explorer heard repeated the word *Katalan-nu*, the words, *Odilia sannu* and *galiva*, the word for healing. The chief went on weaving his story little of which the explorer could understand. When he was finished, the chief turned and addressed something undecipherable to the new *Katalan* seated on the chair of honor. He made a profound bow and hobbled back to his place.

Teeku-mi stood up next, bowed to *Katalan* in the manner of his father, and moving in the front of the altar, commenced his own address to the darkened assembly. Again the explorer heard the story of his healing, and the repetition of all the same words, and then, inevitably, the name of his daughter, *Lunas-nili*. The speech was short and as he returned to his seat, he too made a profound bow to *Katalan.* and with the briefest of looks he let the explorer know of the uncertain hope burning in his father's heart.

The explorer's turn had come. He had to get up and do something. But what? He could not pretend to be a priest, could not engage in sacrilege even if "sacred" was an empty notion as far as anything he knew. Gratefully, just then, a distraction. Two young boys approached the altar carrying lighted candles and two others brought bowls of burning incense. And still another pair came up and placed on the altar a small loaf of bread and a bowl of wine. Then the youths withdrew. Every eye in the torch-lit darkness rested now on the priest figure there on the seat of honor. He had to rise and . . . do what? Looking up desperately at the night sky, moonless and dark, the false priest groaned inwardly for something, someone to wake him from this nightmare.

The explorer got onto his feet, slowly, lugubriously. He affected a bow to *Sabuknu* and moved to the priest's position behind the altar. He had seen priests stand there when he was a curious kid, spying on his altar-boy friends. Now he was behind that altar himself. He peered out into the darkness. Only the front row of native faces were discernible in the torch light of the altar mound. The faces were all fixed on him. Beyond, far out into the night, torch lights flickered unsteadily off the numberless throng, all to a man watching every move he made. Behind, he felt the presence of the chief and *Teeku-mi,* especially *Teeku-mi.* Every aborigine present there that night was waiting. . . . For what? It had been forty years since a priest had stood before them at this altar. Most of them couldn't know any more than he what was supposed to happen next.

As he stood there, the ritualistic tribal sign *Teeku* had taught him flashed into his mind. It struck him now that the ritual resembled the sign of the cross, something the Jesuit must have taught them, perhaps adapting some ritual gesture the *Chiroki* already practiced. It was something he could do. The explorer stretched out both hands above his head, signaling he was about to commence. Then, bowing low, he solemnly touched his forehead and three points across his breast, slowly repeating the ritual three times just as *Teeku* had taught him. As he did this he could feel the quiet, imitative movement of numberless hands in the dark. That worked. And now. . . ?

The explorer looked at the bread and wine cup lying on the altar before him. How could he even go through the motions? He closed his eyes, lowered his head and whispered a plea, likely the first actual prayer that ever escaped his lips. Then, with mental reservations and as much ceremonial solemnity as he could bring himself to fashion, he extended his hands as if to bless the objects on the altar. But then he abruptly froze. Another thought mercifully sprang to mind.

The explorer stepped out from behind the altar and moved up to the edge of the mound. He took out the relic from the pouch around his neck and held it high above his head. Crying out into the night air with all the intensity he could manage, he shouted *Odilia sannu! Odilia sannu!, Odilia sannu!*, repeating the saint's name over and over. Holding out the relic to all quarters, he strode from one side of the altar to the other, vestments swaying, crying out the name of this saint to the farthest reaches of the night. The effect on the throng was immediate. As he shuttled back and forth with the relic above his head, a low chant arose from the darkness, filling the night air. For certain now he heard the Latin words *Ave Verum Corpus* as the chant rose in intensity. They probably had no better idea what this chant really stood for than he did, but it filled the air and eventually took on a life of its own, freeing the explorer to retreat. As he took his seat, breathless, he caught *Teeku-mi* straining forward to study him. The explorer, aglow with relief and his own excitement, threw him a nodding smile, and with that the son of the *Chiroki* chief sank back into his chair and closed his eyes. Matters had changed. Inexplicably, whatever it was that took place on the altar mound just now was having its effect on everyone, including this explorer-turned-priest. And, true enough, strange as it might seem to say this, the explorer too, from that moment on, found himself inexplicably wishing that the miracle *Teeku-mi* was asking of him might truly take place on *dundi lano.* That something as far-fetched as this might really be so.

Sabuknu rose, and with a single gesture silenced the crowd. He began to speak but the explorer would not be listening. His thoughts had drifted back to a priest who had stood before him here on this very mound. The priest who must have sat in the same ceremonial chair and stood before this very altar. And that cryptic message the priest wrote to *Teeku.* How did it go? *Tell Sabuknu I offer my death for them.* The explorer, vested now in the priest's very own garments, caught a glimpse just then of what that message might have meant.

*The relic saves the explorer from an
impossible situation.*

Three days later, in the company of *Teeku-mi,* the explorer set out for *dundi lano.* Before they left, *Sabuknu* took a leopard skin from the pile of skins that made up his throne and gave it to the explorer without a word. As they took their leave, the explorer noticed a small collection of native women gathered at some distance from the chief's dwelling, perhaps fifty of them, of all ages. They were all watching him intently. He could not help but notice that each of the women in this separate group wore a purple scarf, some around the throat or waist, some like a sash across the breast. He remembered seeing one or two women earlier with these purple sashes, but he had never reflected on it. Now their collective presence left him uneasy. Who these women were was not hard to guess. These were the cursed mothers. He wondered if *Teeku-mi's* wife was among them. Curiously, *Teeku-mi* never mentioned anything about the mother of *Lunas-nili,* whatever may have happened to her, even whether she is still living.

The explorer was uneasy about something he wore as well, the saint's relic hanging down from his neck. He was no priest. Nothing of the sort. He only bore the relic because without it he would not be on his way to *dundi cano.* And no anthropologist could dream of any adventure more compelling, more fascinating than this. As he and *Teeku-mi* set out, picking through the jungle brush, more than once he wanted to take the bothersome thing off and shove it in his backpack. But he found he couldn't remove it. Couldn't bring himself to do it. He didn't know why. Perhaps because it was now part of his identity, for the duration. And just possibly what had happened the other night on the altar mound had affected him in some way. He couldn't fathom it, frankly. But one thing was certain. When he got home he would find out all he could about this Saint Odilia, whoever she was (for some reason he knew it was a she).

They had been trekking their way through the brush and undergrowth all day, moving in almost total silence, *Teeku-mi* in front with his backpack (filled with foodstuff for the explorer), and the explorer with his own full backpack keeping up the rear. That night, after they had built a campfire, *Teeku-mi* and the explorer settled down and talked. The aborigine well understood the explorer's limitations with his language, so what they said to each other was elementary in the extreme. The explorer found *Teeku-mi* to be a simple man at heart, very like his uncle, *Teeku,* and had come to like him. The native had been just an infant when *Teeku* left, which would make him around forty years old now. *Teeku-mi* wanted the explorer to tell him about his uncle and it was touching to see how keenly he felt about family. The explorer had no doubt that *Lunas-nili* was topmost on *Teeku-mi's* mind, but neither of them brought up his daughter's name. By now the explorer had figured out what the words *Lunas-nili* meant. He recalled seeing these particular terms on Christopher Damian's vocabulary list. *Lunas* was the word for *berry*, and *nili* meant *sweet*. A nice name and the explorer decided to think of her as Sweet Berry from that point on. From what he had learned earlier, *Teeku-mi's* daughter would be nine years old by now, if she were still alive.

When the explorer asked about his wife, the native

fell silent at first, his gaze seemingly lost in the flames of the campfire. Then, looking up, he said his wife's name was *Tolani*. The few things he added about her were in the past tense, so the explorer assumed she was dead. With gestures as much as words, he said she too had worn the purple sash, like the women there watching them as they took their leave. He told the explorer they are the *masi-Jakareme*, bearers of *Jakareme*, and have to be avoided, even by their husbands. He indicated that sometimes one of them would disappear soon after her child was brought to the mountain. From the way he spoke, the explorer understood that his wife, *Tolani*, was one of those who had vanished and, the explorer guessed, was presumed dead.

Teeku-mi wanted to know if the explorer had children. Since the native didn't realize that priests never marry, the explorer yielded to a bit of dishonesty in hiding behind that rather laboriously made explanation. Actually, he did have a son, but could say practically nothing about him. The boy and his mother had dropped out of his life long ago, or maybe more accurately, *he* had dropped out of theirs. Whatever, it had been nine years since he had had any contact with Charlie. He was a bright boy and was good at languages like his father. The explorer had wanted to call him Chuck but his mother would never hear of it. The boy had to be almost a young man by now. The explorer reflected that he was somewhat of a disaster of a father, not like this aborigine. But that's how it was. Science had become his wife and child.

On their second day out, they arrived on Lost Mountain, on *dundi lano* at last. As they climbed the mountain,

Teeku-mi grew quite tense and kept his spear at the ready all day. The explorer sensed him fighting quiet terror in his heart. That night at the campfire the native kept the fire burning bright. To ease the tension, the explorer asked him how he would recognize Sweet Berry. *Teeku-mi* pointed to the left side of his forehead and from his few words the explorer pieced together that his daughter had a red, berry-like birthmark on that side of her brow. Beyond that the native remained silent.

They rose early the next day and by late morning they reached their destination, the depot or drop-off point for the *Jakareme* infants. Not long after, the son of the *Chiroki* chief departed, leaving the explorer there alone. They had an agreement that the explorer would have nine days on the mountain. Nine days, he surmised, should be enough to gather the sort of data he needed.

Happily, *Sabuknu* had had the explorer's things brought up from the river, so he had everything he'd need with him now. Apart from foodstuff and items like frying pan, etc., he brought a quantity of medical and pharmaceutical supplies, thinking he might be able to do something helpful for these poor souls, assuming of course that a deaf and blind colony had actually ever really formed itself on this mountain, and that he would be able to find them. If there were a settlement of the deaf and blind on this mountain, the wonder is how they could have managed to survive.

The explorer had also taken a voice recorder with him. He planned to capture detailed impressions of the nine days he had before him, more or less as they occurred.

CHAPTER EIGHT

ON LOST MOUNTAIN

Daisy here again. The following account was transcribed from audio tapes that, according to my father, had fallen into his hands. He never explained to me how he obtained these tapes. In them, the explorer records his mysterious adventures on dundi lano.

DAY ONE: ENCOUNTER WITH THE *JAKAREME*

IT WAS LATE MORNING when we broke into this little clearing where I'm now standing. I seem to be on a large, verdant plateau still some ways below the summit of *dundi lano*. This clearing is basically a large, flat outcropping of rock, hemmed in on all sides by dense jungle flora. As I understand it, this is the drop-off point. I gather that the *Chiroki,* when they bring the children here, never go beyond this point. What lies beyond it is the big question I am to answer. But the babies they deposit here all disappear, so someone is out there. It's possible it could be animals of course.

In the center of the rock clearing are three small circles made of stones. The center circle I take it is for the deaf-blind child. It is quite small and the stones forming it are large, making a sort of crib. The child would be placed there, probably bound also so as to restrain its movements.

The diameter of the second circle is larger and its floor is covered with ashes. I suspect this is how they try to signal their presence to the *Jakareme*. Early this morning, as we made our way up here through the undergrowth, *Teeku-mi* began collecting a large number of branches from eucalyptus bushes. As soon as we arrived here, he placed wood and kindling in this circle and then smothered them with these branches. The pungent smell of burning eucalyptus tells the *Jakareme* a child has been brought. At least that's the idea. *Teeku-mi* did not light the fire. He left it up to me how to make contact with these people.

In the third rock circle, the smallest, *Teeku-mi* placed the few gifts he brought up with him—a clay water pitcher, a clay cup, and a knife in a leather holster. He sped through these chores with uncanny haste. When he was done, he came up to me, touched *Odilia sannu* hanging down on my chest, bowed low, said something I could not get, and quickly ran off. Then for the briefest of moments he looked back and in the black, fearful eyes of this native I saw flash a brief, fleeting glance of hope, imperious hope. I confess that glance rather haunts me, like an unwanted obligation. I try to erase it from my mind but find I cannot. I am only too aware that he and I have very different reasons for my coming here.

And so I am alone now at this child-drop, standing here as I dictate this, figuring out what to do next. If I light the fire and there are people out there, I assume someone will show up before long, however they manage to do it. But they'll find no child. They will not see me of course, being blind, but they'll know someone has come and they won't know why. Not the way to start things off. Wait. . . .

I just noticed a break in the thickets that encircle this clearing. There is a young kapok tree and I see a vine wrapped around it. I'm over to it now. The vine leads back into the jungle, strung out waist-high from one tree to the next along what looks to be a footpath. It's quite overgrown and barely discernible but this is encouraging. There are *Jakareme* out there in this jungle, and this is how they feel their way to the depot.

I've been tracing this vine line for almost an hour now. But for this waist-high guideline, you would hardly know there was a trail. Obviously not used very often. Interesting though, every so often there is a smaller vine with a sequence of knots dangling from the main vine. Very likely coded road signs, for people who can only get where they're going by feel.

Hold on, there's something just off the path to my right. . . .

What caught my eye are parts of a human skeleton, strewn about just a few yards from the line. The skeleton is dismembered, torn apart by what must have been a pretty good-sized animal. It's of a youngster, maybe no more than fourteen or so, lying here undisturbed for probably a year, judging from the condition. No doubt these poor souls make easy prey for animals on this mountain. The deafblind victim would not know what was coming at him until he felt its teeth. And of course it could have been a young girl. A bit beyond Sweet Berry's age, I would say. . . .

I must be getting close to the *Jakareme* settlement, or whatever it is that constitutes their living arrangement. The path I've been on for a while now is more of a trail, wider and matted down with travel. In place of a single vine line, there are now separate, sturdier liana vines bordering each edge of the trail, like guardrails on a country road. And here and there the trail intersects with other trails and paths. These crossroads all have those small roadside vines dangling with their variously spaced knots. It would be a linguist's dream to decipher these knot codes, if one only had the time.

I hear something coming. . . .

I am looking at my first *Jakareme* this very instant. Four males are coming down the trail towards me. I've ducked into the brush, only a few yards away from them as they approach, but it's clear they can't see me, or hear my voice as I record this. They are in some sort of formation, two in front, two behind, moving at times with heads held at odd angles in the manner of the blind. In appearance they are gaunt, starkly so, with open but utterly vacant eyes, eyes that look normal but see nothing. Whatever genetic condition they suffer from does not disfigure them in any obvious way. They have the unmistakable bronze coloration of the *Chiroki*. And like the *Chiroki*, all are beardless. The two in front are older, perhaps in their early forties. The two behind are in their teens. They appear to have empty reed sacks around their waist; the youth in the back are carrying coils of vine. I suspect this is a work detail, off to collect food most likely. It's very interesting. They all have short, cane-like poles. One in front uses his pole to probe the ground, the one next to him regularly swings his pole out

The explorer encounters his first Jakareme *on Lost Mountain.*

in lazy figure-eight movements. The youths in the rear rest theirs on the shoulders of the two in front, keeping the group intact. I notice that the near end of each pole, the end closest to their hands, is sharpened to a fine point. Swung around, it makes an effective weapon. For fending off animals very likely.

I've been following them down a branch off the main trail. One in the front seems to be the leader. He keeps one hand in touch with the guide line. Every now and then he stops to read the dangling knot signs. The others react instantly to each of his stops and starts. From the looks of it, this drill has been undergone countless times before. . . .

The vine path has led us to a small grove of fruit trees where they stop. These look to be a species of plum trees laden with fruit. The four are placing vine around their waists and tying the lines to each other. All four are now tethered together like a chain. The lead man has tied his line to the tree that serves as the all-important link back to the trail.

Now they've moved into the grove and are on their hands and knees, feeling around for fallen fruit. One is tugging on the line to let the others know he's made a find. The wine-colored, plum-like fruit look like oversized plutots. There's plenty on the ground that they miss, often just by inches, and I am tempted to nudge plums into their hands. But I think better of it. They swing their arms and cane poles around quite deftly, like feelers.

I just picked one from a tree. It tasted tart but not unpleasant.

One of the youngsters climbs the tree and is shaking its branches. He signals for the others with a line pull.

They come and shake the tree also and grope for the fallen fruit. Slowly, methodically, they are filling their sacks. Their movements seem routinized as if they had been doing this all their lives. . . .

They've been at this for an hour. Their reed sacks are full and they're making ready to go back on the trail.

We're on the main trail now heading back in the direction we came from, and we've just run into two males coming toward us. They are approaching side-by-side in the usual formation, one with his seeing-eye pole swinging out ahead, the other probing the ground in front. The lead poles of the two teams collide and we all abruptly halt. The encounter must be a common occurrence for no one acts surprised.

Our team is moving aside now to let the others pass. I see palms stretched out for greetings and fingers reaching for tiny creeper vines hanging from the neck. They all have them. It must be how they identify themselves. I don't want to get too close but it looks like there are as many as three or four such strings dangling from the neck, of different lengths, all with these little knots. As they pass I notice some, after reading the knots, reach for a face or a shoulder, like you would when recognizing a friend.

What is so unearthly about this meet-up is the absence of any sound. Total utter silence. I can only try to imagine what blindness is like, but this silence is something you can hear. You literally experience it, as if you too were deaf. Not strange that coastal rumors talk about the silence. The silence will take some getting used to.

The two have passed by and we move on. . . .

We've come upon a good-sized brook blocking the

trail and are turning to follow the trail upstream along its bank. . . . We're at a crossover point now where the vine line stretches across to the far side. Here the brook is only ankle deep and is fordable, but the brook bed looks green with slimy rocks and the crossing is going to be tricky even for someone with vision. . . .

One of the teenagers just stumbled into the water. All his fruit has spilled out and is drifting off. His cane-pole also. I have to help. . . .

He's OK now. I grabbed the cane-pole and thrust it into his hands. He was too stunned to know what was happening. And I managed to get most of the fruit back into his sack before they floated off. The others struggled to get him on his feet and in the melee one of them walked right into me. It startled him but there was enough confusion for him not to make anything of it.

The four are now making their way along the trail across from me on the brook's other side. I did not im-mediately cross over with them as their trail seems to parallel the brook and the little path I am on. I will have no trouble observing them from my side and a little separation like this affords me a better view of where all this is leading. I can keep them in sight and, if need be, I have my binoculars.

We've been heading downstream now for a while. I see that the land along the far side is grassy with little clusters of bamboo groves here and there. Back behind them about a hundred yards a bluff rises almost vertical-ly running parallel to the brook. At its base I see some caves and overhangs. With a fresh, running brook on one side and a protective bluff on the other, this particular tract seems made to order for a settlement. I wonder how the *Jakareme* could possibly have selected it.

The men with their sack loads of fruit are moving more quickly. We must be getting close to their colony.

CHAPTER NINE

THE *JAKAREME* DETECT THE
EXPLORER'S PRESENCE

I AM LOOKING THROUGH my binoculars at the *Jakareme* settlement, such as it is, spread out barely fifty yards across the brook from where I am standing. There's not very much to it. I walked on my side of the brook from one end of this settlement to the other and basically all I see is a string of crude shelters set up in bamboo groves. Most have several *Jakareme* in them, all seemingly busy at one thing or another. There are 17 of these little structures, if you can call them that, basically just crude roofs, made from vines strung out between tree trunks. Branches and heaps of thatched grass are strewn across the vines for overhead covering. There are no sides, except for a single vine line, nothing in the way of doors or entrances, and on the inside I see nothing but rough bamboo flooring, what looks like bamboo poles laid out and strung together. The shelters are linked to each other via the main trail that tracks along the brook. Vine paths off the trail lead up to each of these dwellings.

In all I have counted so far seventy-four *Jakareme,* either in these shelters or feeling their way along the brook trail. A few were in the water, washing themselves or whatever. There may be others out on the jungle

Legend

1 - Main trail leading to the settlement.

2 - Brook cross-over point.

3 - Trail continues along brook to settlement. Paths off this trail lead to individual dwellings.

4 - Brook paralleling the main settlement trail.

5 - Explorer's camp-site.

6 - Chief's dwelling with assembly courtyard before it.

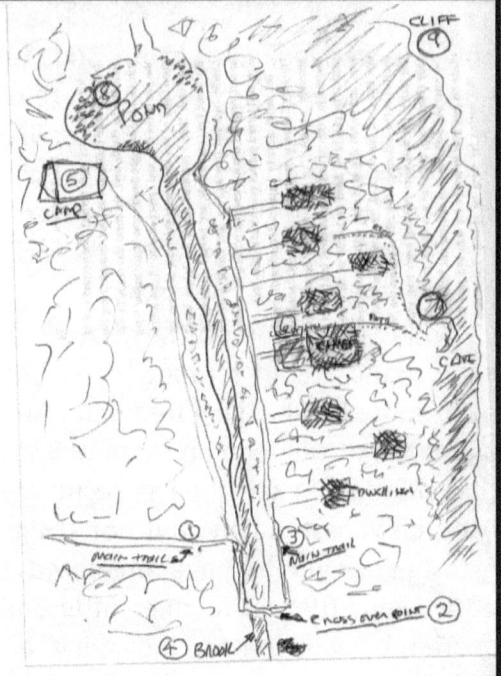

7 – Cave located within bluff that parallels the settlement. Note the paths leading to the cave from the chief's dwelling and from another of the dwellings on the women's side of the encampment.

8 – The pond, with lily pads along its edges.

9 - Cliff that parallels the brook. Together, cliff and brook provide natural protection for the *Jakareme* settlement.

Map of the Jakareme *settlement, hand-drawn by the explorer.*

trails and paths gathering food. I see all ages, although only one who looked truly old, and most are fairly young. All the *Jakareme* are extremely thin and gaunt in appearance. The men are beardless, like all *Chiroki* males. Generally they do not look sickly but through my glass I see evidence of their hard life—scars from injuries, skin rashes, here and there some festering sores. Their expressions are uniformly empty.

What sort of life do they have? The only world they know hands them scrapes, cuts, banged toes, a blow from some low-hanging tree limb. And there are preying animals that can leap on them out of nowhere. And yet, they don't strike me at all as desperate or even troubled. A bit downcast maybe, but not struggling. Not at all. In fact they seem to have organized themselves rather effectively. They have their little shelters all interconnected by vine paths, indicating an organized social order. And the industry of the settlement is immediately obvious. I see no one just lying around. They rather give an impression of busy ants, everyone doing some little piece of work for the benefit of the colony. Through my glass I see women chopping what looks like greens of some kind. In another shelter I see a woman bathing a child, and elsewhere men stripping vines. And men out on the trails, no small number of them, likely seeking the community's next meal.

Interestingly, I see no mixed gender arrangements in any of these shelters. Males are exclusively with males on one side of the colony, females on the other. I also observe an elderly male in a shelter at the very center of the camp, considerably larger than any of the others. I suspect this individual is the colony's *Sabuknu*.

A sprinkling of children of all ages are spread throughout, boys with the men except for the very young, girls with the women. I've yet to see a girl that looks nine years old, Sweet Berry's age. One can't assume she is still alive. From what I see from the mean age, life expectancy here is quite short.

Tomorrow I will cross over and see about making contact. Right now I need to set up camp for myself, further downstream well beyond the trail lines. If the wind is right, I can build a fire without risking detection. And I need to rinse out these clothes I have on. The *Jakareme* sense of smell has to be quite acute. But before anything else, I'm going to go back to the child-drop and pick up my backpack. And the backpack *Teeku-mi* carried up with foodstuff and the gifts *Sabuknu* gave me just before we left.

DAY TWO

Late afternoon yesterday, after I retrieved my things, I found a nice spot well downstream where the brook spreads out into a pond. The pond is positively loaded with what looks to me like a variety of silver carp. I built myself a little lean-to and was getting ready to net one of these good-eating critters for supper when four *Jakareme* males showed up on the far side. They had primitive vine nets slung over their shoulders. I watched them as they tethered themselves together and waded out into the water. Two were older and seemed to know how to cast their nets, the other two were teenagers and more than once their nets got tangled with the tether lines. It was interesting to witness the patience of the older pair as they felt around to untangle the mess.

All their movements are slow and deliberate, without any sign of frustration or anxiety despite their handicaps.

They were not netting much fish and I decided to help them out. I have a light fishing net with me and in the space of half an hour caught more of these carp than the four of them combined. I kept dumping my catch into the reed basket they kept at the pond's edge, and as they got ready to leave, the basket load clearly startled them.

Earlier this morning I made plans to cross over and enter their colony. I went upstream to ford across in the shallows, and as I neared the spot, I heard strange whimpering sounds. There at the edge of the brook a young *Jakareme* lad lay writhing in the water. I waded out to him and found that his arm was broken just below the elbow. It was sticking out at a crazy angle, but luckily the skin was not punctured. Probably he had been bringing up the rear of some procession when he slipped on the rock slime. No one heard the splash of course and those ahead of him must have gone on for some time before they realized he was not with them. And when they did, how could they find him?

I dragged the youth onto the bank and tried to make him comfortable while I ran back to get my first-aid kit. Fortunately for him, my father was a general practitioner and as a kid I used to sit in his office and watch him. I even thought I might become a doctor myself, so I do know a thing or two about setting bones. I gave the lad a shot of morphine, which startled him but quieted him down enough to let me get at the arm. The poor kid had no idea who was handling him or what I was trying to do. But we got through it. I put a makeshift splint on his arm and wrapped it well with heavy gauze. Then I literally carried him across the brook. Not easy given the rock slime but I at least could see. As I carried him, he felt for the identification vines that he expected would be hanging down from my neck. What he found of course was *Odilia sannu* in her snakeskin pouch, something wholly unrecognizable. I could feel his body stiffen.

Once on the far side, I put him down, placed his good hand in contact with the trail's vine line and let him go. I don't think he had any idea where he was but the moment he touched the vine he knew what to do. He felt his way along until he came across a dangling trail marker, telling him exactly which way to go. And off he went, with me not far behind, feeling his way downstream in the direction of the settlement.

It wasn't long before he ran into a team coming toward him on the trail in the usual echelon formation. The boy had lost his own cane-pole in the brook but a swinging pole of the approaching party struck his shoulder and everyone froze. Feeling for his vine necklace, the leader understood at once who he was. Possibly this group had been sent out to look for him as the encounter led to considerable animation. Everyone had to touch him. All this was happening with me standing just a few yards off. Then I saw the boy tracing something on the lead man's palm. Clearly this is how they communicate, and undoubtedly the boy was relating what had happened. This got relayed to eager palms thrust out to grasp what was going on. And each had to feel the splinted arm. The unfamiliar splint and gauze bandaging were puzzling. And that someone unknown helped the boy this way had to be confounding. You could tell from the flurry of their palming that what the lad had to say was stirring them up. Yet, for all the animation in their bodies, their faces stayed as empty and vacant as ever.

My curiosity about this palming drew me in closer than I should have and I wound up brushing against one of the party. This contact from an unexpected direction startled the native, even more so when I scooted back and his instinctive pole probe struck nothing but empty space. For sure, my introduction mustn't come about by bumping into them this way. That will only make them wary and close them off from me. How the *Jakareme* communicate—without benefit of sight or sound—is the reason I came up the river. For sure I won't get very far just peeking over their shoulders, but how do I get into their lives, without alarming them even more than I already have. I wonder if it is even possible for them to accept someone so unlike them. Do they know they are blind and deaf? How could they? That there are people like me who see and hear, who live in a world they can-not even imagine – that there is a sky overhead with clouds, that birds fly in that sky and sing, that there are such things as daylight and moonlight. What can they know other than the objects they can touch, or taste and smell? They have each other, of course, but what will they make of someone nor tethered to anyone, who comes and goes as he wishes. Someone who does unim-aginable things? *Unimaginable things.* Oddly, that night on the altar mound flashed through my mind just then. That was unimaginable. Then I thought of *Teeku-mi's*

Sweet Berry. As far as he's concerned, I'm here chiefly for his daughter, to cure her, speaking of unimaginable things!

The formation has turned around making its way with the boy back toward the settlement, with me trailing alongside. Progress is slow. We keep running into other teams, and the same ritual of palming has had to be repeated. By now as many as twenty *Jakareme* men and boys are strung out behind on the trail. I've been keeping to the grass just outside the vine lines, using the time to record these events up to this point. Interestingly, I've yet to see a woman anywhere on the trails. . . .

We are now entering the settlement. Every hundred feet or so I see a path branch off from the main trail up to a little bamboo grove. And in its midst there's a primitive shelter strung up between tree trunks, some closer to the brook, others farther back toward the bluff.

We've arrived at the larger shelter I spoke of yesterday, located in the center of the camp. The leader of this procession turns into it, with all the rest falling in behind. This I am fairly certain is the dwelling of the chief, the local *Sabuknu*. In front of his shelter is a grassy clearing forming a natural courtyard. It's fascinating to watch this: the incoming vine path subdivides into five parallel vine paths, leading up to the chief's shelter like fingers to the palm of a hand. The natives coming off the trail have distributed themselves along these fingers. . . .

Right now I'm standing just a few feet outside the

chief's enclosure. Inside I see an elderly man with four others, perhaps the chief's underlings although one of them seems quite young. The shelter has no sides apart from a vine line, only a thatched roof and rough flooring. This floor is made of bamboo poles laid out and roped together with thin vines. The lead man has stepped onto the flooring and those inside instantly react. At this point, of course, those inside the shelter have no idea of the procession that has formed before them. The new-comer identifies himself by tapping on the bamboo flooring. One of the underlings taps back a coded re-sponse. The chief stands up. He's stretching out his right palm with that swaying, figure-eight motion that substi-tutes for vision here. The old chief looks like all the others in this camp, gaunt and thin as wire. He is tall and despite his age, he stands erect like one accustomed to command. . . .

The two have made physical contact and are greeting each other. It's fascinating to see this. The arrival sweeps his four finger tips across the chief's palm twice, a ges-ture that is instantly returned. Now they have started palming in earnest.

Given all the activity, I don't think I'll risk disclosing my presence if I enter the dwelling. I want to observe how they communicate. Judging from the hand move-ments their conversation has become particularly animated. . . .

Now the boy with the broken arm is being brought forward by a lad his own age, probably a buddy. The chief's fingers are taking in the splint and cloth binding. He turns to relay what he has learned onto the palms of the youngest of the four underlings. This youth runs his fingers along the boy's arm, then turns and begins palming the underling nearest him, and this underling in turn does the same. What the chief has said then gets passed to the one closest in the courtyard. Like ripples in a pond, each turns to spread the word to the one behind him.

You can't tell anything from the chief's face but his body movements say he is clearly troubled. He, after all, is the community's guide, even very likely its wisdom, and now something well beyond his understanding has taken place. What is he to make of it? What wise counsel can he give? He must certainly have grasped that there's another world somewhere, a world he and his people know nothing about. A world that every once in a great while delivers them a baby. And leaves behind dishes and blades that they could never fashion on their own. So he knows that his world is not all there is. But whatever else there is lies far away. Now this has changed. What happened with the boy this morning happened right in his lap so to speak. And what happened at the pool yesterday—the inexplicable quantity of fish—must surely have gotten reported. And with today's event the chief surely knows some presence from that alien world has entered his camp. It's my job now to make sure he doesn't take that as a threat, not to him personally nor to his community. How to do this is what I have to figure out, and soon, if this incredible opportunity is not to be wasted.

The chief and two of his underlings, including the youngest, have just left the shelter from the rear and are feeling their way along a vine that leads through the bamboo grove up to the bluff behind. I am following them

The explorer follows the boy he aided into the shelter of the local Jakareme *chief.*

as I speak. I see there's a cave at the base of the bluff, just ahead of us. It has a crude roof structure over its entrance. I cannot see inside and can't tell how deep it is. The chief has gone into the cave alone, and the two underlings have taken up positions at the entrance. I have my flashlight with me and would follow him inside, but the entrance is narrow and I am not entirely sure I can get by these underlings undetected. . . .

I've been waiting near the cave entrance for fifteen minutes, but the chief is still in there. I'm going back down to the compound. . . .

I'm back at the compound now. The assembly has disbanded, and the chief's other two underlings are making for the main trail. I'm following them as they feel along the vine upstream. . . .

The two just turned up into the first shelter off the trail. I'm only a few feet away now. One of them an-nounces their visit by tapping on the bamboo flooring. Now he is palming the male who came forward. There are others in the shelter as well, all with swaying, out-stretched hands. The palming will take some time, but I can see this is a ritual that will be repeated again and again. Before the day is over every *Jakareme* in the settlement will know of these events and what the chief has to say about them.

I've been exploring the main trail, keeping well ahead of the chief's two emissaries, getting a closer look at how this settlement has organized itself. As I mentioned, the shelters where we are now, upstream from the chief's compound, are for males exclusively. There are exactly ten of these shelters, each housing four males as far as I can tell, one or two who are older, mostly in their thirties or forties, the others younger including some who are just boys. I see no one who is truly old with the exception of the tribe's chief.

The shelters downstream from the chief's compound are for women, the part of the camp I've yet to explore. But from the other side of the brook yesterday I counted seven female shelters. The women and children are of all ages also, but again, none of the women are what you would call old and a good many are young. I have yet to learn if Sweet Berry is there among them. . . .

LATER

I've now made a fairly thorough inspection of the male quarters. It appears all these shelters serve as little guilds, performing some function for the whole tribe. As noted, each typically has four members, the two who are older and the younger two who are probably apprentices. Gathering and preparing food looks to be the principal work for many of these guilds. A little while ago I saw four *Jakareme* males bringing in sack loads of figs to a shelter that appears to function as a food storage center. As soon as this echelon announced themselves, those present in this shelter came forward and formed a chain with them. Figs were passed along this chain out to a sunlit clearing to the side of the shelter. There a native systematically laid the fruit out on a sun-drenched ledge. Rows of these figs were already drying there in the sun. Another rock ledge nearby was blanketed with berries. Inside the enclosure I saw reed baskets heaped with raisins.

Another shelter nearby had baskets filled with various kinds of nuts. Two of the males there were cracking shells and pounding kernels into a fine powder. Still another guild down the trail was busy mashing grapes. It will be interesting to know if they ferment it.

One of these guilds specializes in fishing. I recognized the fishermen from the first day at the pond. At the moment they were mending vine nets. In the bamboo grove right next to them another guild was filleting carp from a recent catch. They had blades for this work. Blades that had to have been brought here with babies.

From what I observe, most of the food gathered is consumed that day, but some is set aside for sun-drying. In the off-season, the *Jakareme* must have to live on dried fruit and nuts, along with storable vegetables like wild onions and roots. And no doubt filleted carp, dried or otherwise.

These male guilds do other things too, of course, like collecting creepers, vines and lianas from trees, and maintaining the guide lines on the trail. Another guild is concerned with harvesting and drying reeds for baskets, which it appears they also weave. But the majority of the males are involved in gathering and storing food. Luckily it's not too difficult for them to do this. The area has an abundance of edible roots, wild vegetables, different sorts of fruits and nuts, to say nothing of the plentiful carp. One wonders if the Lost Mountain somehow isn't making it up to the *Jakareme*, for they could not survive were this mountain any less generous in its offerings. So much for *dundi lano's* "evil spirits."

I am now on the women's side of the camp. The women's guilds are different. As I noted earlier, women are rarely to be met with on the trails. Their principal work is the community's meals. Men bring them the raw materials, the roots, leeks, edible plant leaves, fish fillets, whatever. The women prepare it. They have for their purposes a good quantity of clay cups, bowls and chopping blades. These artifacts look like they have been accumulating for generations, precious artifacts no doubt even outlasting the infants they originally accompanied.

All food is eaten raw, understandably, since they could never handle fire and probably have no familiarity with it. Some items, like roots and tubers of various kinds, are soaked in water and left out in the heat of the sun to soften, likely for days. Just a little while ago I watched the women in one guild preparing a meal. First they felt their way out to a shallow pool by their compound to retrieve a quantity of gnarled roots that had been soaking. Then they skinned the roots and finely chopped them. They added seeds, cut up quantities of leaves and fruit and some kind of juice and readied the mixture in bowls for distribution. I take it this will be for the tribe's noon meal. More than one of the women's shelters is engaged this way in preparing meals.

Right now, for example, I'm looking at a guild nearby that specializes in readying fish. They have a crude solar oven set up in a little clearing just outside their shelter. The oven is put together from silicone-rich stones, and extends several yards in length. The sun on the mountainside here is quite intense and given enough time this sort of stone will reflect sufficient heat to actually bake fish. Fish fillets are slowly baking on it as I speak. I expect this particular guild may be preparing the community's supper. Interestingly though, there seems to be hardly enough fillets on the oven for everyone.

The community appears to eat only twice a day, just before noon and just before sunset.

Men do not seem to come over to the women's side of the settlement. There must be a taboo about that, except for the chief's four underlings. Just a little while ago these four came to pick up the food prepared by the women's guilds and distribute it to shelters on both sides of the camp. These four very obviously are how the chief exercises his authority. Some in this community will have baked fish tonight and some won't. I wonder how such things get decided.

I have yet to see any woman in the men's sector. Settlement taboos again. And even these underbosses, when they come into the women's section for the meals, never actually step inside the shelters. They tap on the flooring and the women bring them the food in bowls stacked on top of each other. To say the least, the fare is meager, but I've seen the men on the trails eating berries and nuts. Perhaps these are somehow shared with the women as well. They're all quite thin, men and women alike, but no one strikes me as seriously undernourished exactly.

Women perform other tasks as well. For example, and rather remarkably under the circumstances, there's a women's guild that appears responsible for clothing the entire *Jakareme* community. The men in the camp have a simple loin cloth around the waist, the women wear crude, loose-fitting, sleeveless gowns. From what I see, the four women of this little guild fashion these garments from plant fibers. I cannot identify the plant but it bears some resemblance to flax. What they produce is crude, to be sure, but that they have learned how to make yarn from plant fiber and then to weave cloth and fashion garments is nothing short of stunning. Obviously, for all their handicaps, there's no shortage of smarts in this camp. I can't even imagine the patience it must have taken to figure these matters out. How many generations of *Jakareme* did it require?

Let me describe what I've seen. It's really quite remarkable. Alongside this guild's shelter is a small field strewn with the stems of these flax-like plants, all carefully trimmed of roots and leaves. That's the first step, turning green stems into straw under the rays of the sun.

As I see it, the next step takes place down at the water. There's a shallow little pond right off the brook that has been loaded with this straw. The women are letting the straw soak until it literally rots—the technical term for this is retting—allowing the soft plant fibers to be separated from the stem's woody part. The women then spin these fibers by hand, twisting and twirling the fibers into a coarse thread and knotting the ends together to make balls of yarn.

What I've been observing as I speak is the step that happens next. They have set up crude looms on the floor of their shelter, basically just a series of pegs wedged into the bamboo flooring and spaced in the desired shape and size (in the present case, that of a women's gown). As I speak I am watching busy hands wind and weave the yarn, back and forth, in and out across this loom, with knots everywhere to firm the fabric up. It must take these women weeks if not months to produce a single garment like this. When finished this will become a gown that no sighted woman could ever bring herself to wear. But it's functional and the flax-like fabric looks to be soft and comfortable enough. Interestingly, I saw no one in the entire camp not wearing minimal clothing. One wonders why that is so. The climate does not call for covering, except at night, and obviously there's no visual need for modesty. An anthropological puzzle my academic peers would no doubt relish pondering.

I've also spotted several women's guilds further downstream concerned with children. These are probably schools. And this could be where I'll find Sweet Berry. I've spotted several young girls around her age but it's already too late in the day to pursue this now. I will look into it tomorrow. What I am to do with her, assuming I find her here, escapes me. For one, the genders here are not allowed to mix, so this will pose a problem once these women sense the presence of a man. But the real issue of course is *Teeku-mi's* impossible expectations. What in the world am I to do with that?

The sun is close to setting and I should cross over to my camp. I haven't eaten all day and my garments could stand a rinsing, lest my presence gets announced despite myself.

CHAPTER TEN

THE EXPLORER BECOMES
ONE OF THEM

DAY THREE

A S I HALF EXPECTED, after the incident with the boy's arm yesterday morning the mood of the community has changed. Late afternoon yesterday as I made my way back to my little camp here, I noticed all the males on the trail had the sharp tip of their cane-poles pointing outward. I saw nothing like that the first day. And all afternoon there was coming and going at the chief's compound, far more than I remember witnessing the day before. On the way I came upon the chief's four underbosses distributing the evening meal. What struck me was the jumpy way they were swinging their cane-poles, as if half-expecting to run into the alien. It half-amuses me to think that it's me they are fearful of. But it's a bit unsettling too.

How am I to get on a good footing with these people? We can't communicate. And everything I do tends to spook them. Yet it won't be good enough to keep out of their way, watching with this recorder in hand. I have to get into their heads, to some extent at least, and find out what the life of the *Jakareme* is like on the inside. No account would be worth much without it. And if I can I'd like to help these poor people too, in some way. And then there's *Teeku-mi's* Sweet Berry. I should know soon enough if his daughter is still alive. I confess I still have no idea what I'm to do if and when I find her.

I pondered these matters virtually all night and I've come to a solid conclusion. If I am to enter into the life of this community there is only one course to take: I have to become a *Jakareme*. I need to go around with a cane-pole, do palm greetings and have them experience me as no different from them. Yes, of course, inevitably I'll be seen as different. I don't know their language, for one, and I have a beard and the clothes I wear are different. And inevitably I'll do things that will startle them. Most likely they will take me for a visitor from that other world. The mature ones here certainly must wonder about this other world—why it delivers babies and useful objects—but however they imagine it, they can't have any idea of how different it is, what it means to see, to hear, to be free to come and go outside the vine lines.

This morning first thing upon rising I made a cane-pole for myself. I even sharpened one end. We'll see what happens now. . . .

Just moments ago on the trail I passed my first test as a *Jakareme*. A team of four food-gatherers were on their way out with empty reed sacks over their shoulders. The lead male was weaving his cane-pole in figure eights before him as they came toward me, sharp point out. I swung my pole into his and with that we all stopped. The lead male reached out and I made the standard greeting, just as I've seen it done, drawing the tips of my fingers quickly across his palm twice, followed by two quick taps. He did the same. I reached for his necklace, the coded creeper vines they hang around their necks to identify each other, and he reached for mine. What he fingered of course was the snakeskin pouch containing the relic and needless to say it stopped him cold. *Teeku's* ring on my finger puzzled him too, as did my soft, machine-made shirt when he realized I was not bare-skinned (as they are). He reached for my face and drew back when he found my beard. He knew he had run into the alien. I was confusingly different but I was friendly and we had greeted in the proper way. And he knew I had done a good thing for the boy's arm. So he began to relax a bit.

This ritual had to be solemnly repeated with the others. Each fingered the snakeskin pouch and felt my shirt and my beard, and to a man they seemed intrigued with the hard object on my finger. They too tried palming me and my inability to respond clearly perplexed them. I'm not like them, yet not entirely alien. A puzzle to be pondered later, but right now they had work to do, so in very short order they moved on. . . .

I've had similar encounters like this all morning, all going pretty much in the way described earlier. By now the entire community must know that the alien in their midst is not threatening. They understand I say very little and have hair on my face and have this curious hard object as my identification string, and a strange, hard circle on one of my fingers. But this alien has done some good things and so far has harmed no one. So I'm becoming accepted, more or less. It's funny, though, when

I think about it. This is the second time *Odilia sannu* has changed my identity, just at the point where I needed to be seen in a new way entirely. First she made me a priest and now here I am a *Jakareme*. . . .

A little while ago, as I was walking along the main settlement trail that tracks parallel to the brook, I spotted the youth with the broken arm. He was sitting in a shelter in one of the shady bamboo groves just off the trail. There was an older native bending over him, like a father over an injured son. That's how the two struck me at any rate. I wanted to go in and see how his arm was doing but there is a strict protocol about entering any shelter. I couldn't simply barge in. By now I've figured out that the practice is to announce yourself by tapping your identity code on the bamboo floor, letting the vibrations inform those inside who has come. Those inside respond in kind, letting the visitor know who is home to receive him. These conventions are fundamental to their life. The *Jakareme* do not easily abide an unexpected touch from an unidentified source.

I made up a code for myself on the spot: two taps, three taps, a pause and then two rapid taps. The two did not recognize these taps of course but the older man tapped back anyway, got up and held out his hand in that standard swaying fashion. I did the same and we went through the business of touching vine tags, etc. He fingered the snakeskin pouch and my shirt and so knew right away I was the mysterious alien who had tended the boy's broken arm. He was especially friendly, grateful I suppose for the help given his young protégé. At any rate he took my hand and couched it in both of his. It was a warm, unexpected gesture. I decided to give him a name and to do this for others too, to keep them sorted in my mind. This fellow is now my second Damian, Damian-Two, because he seems like a very decent guy.

I looked at the boy's arm. The arm had swollen and was causing him some discomfort which I relieved by loosening the bandaging. Otherwise the arm looked good. I am going to call him Carlito-Two, for he and Carlito are about the same age and build.

I noticed that Damian-Two had some nasty looking scratches along the sides of both legs, most likely from some thick briar patch he had gotten himself into. I keep my medical kit with me now, and soon as I touched his leg he seemed to understand. The alcohol made him wince, but I cleaned the wounds and applied an antibiotic ointment. Afterwards, he took my hand and began palming a message. Nothing of what he was saying got through to me, of course. The only response I could make was to brush a single finger twice across his inside wrist, the way I've seen it done, conveying what I guess signifies *good*, *OK*, or something positive of that nature. Little did I realize what it was I was agreeing to. . . .

For the last several hours Damian-Two has been taking me to *Jakareme* in one shelter after another, all with wounds, body sores, or other health problems. I treated each of them as best I could. A few were feverish and all I could do was give them aspirin.

The morning's experience got me inside the community, at least its male part. A few of them, especially the younger ones, were responsive and even grateful for what I was doing for them, but the older ones are mostly uneasy. A few with skin problems would not let me touch them, Damian-Two's ministrations notwithstanding. It's unfortunate. Some of these sores are nasty and need attention. . . .

By now we have been to virtually every shelter on the male side of the camp, finally ending up in front of the chief's enclosure. Two males are standing by the vine line that leads into the little courtyard. The sharp points of their cane-poles are pointing outward. Damian-Two certainly knows where he is, but he does not try to enter. How he understood the entrance is barred escapes me. The *Jakareme* seem to have a sixth sense about these things. . . .

Damian-Two has just left. He took my hand and palmed goodbye. As far as I can tell, *goodbye* is similar to the gesture for *hello* except that here the fingertips are swept across the palm three times instead of twice, followed by a single tap, all done more slowly. Then suddenly the native cupped my hand between his for long seconds. I gather it means *thank you,* or even perhaps, if done with enough tenderness, something more affectionate, possibly even a form of love. I think I named Damian-Two rather well. . . .

I can see the chief from where I'm standing, up there in his compound. He's alone with one of his underlings, the youngest of the four, the one he always seems to be with. I'm going to call this youngster Charlie-Two, as he's about the age of my son. The chief seems very much to favor him. Right now they're palming away. Doubtless the chief by now knows all about these activities of mine. I suspect they don't sit too well with him. Anything big like this that is not under his control can't be to his liking, even if it benefits the community. I realize now it was a mistake not to seek his blessing before getting this involved with his people, behind his back so to speak. At least that's the way he's apt to see it. A very big mistake on my part. How to approach him now will take some skillful finessing. My project for tomorrow.

Today, in what's left of it, I want to go into the women's side of this camp and scout out Sweet Berry, if she's here. I'd better do this now just in case the chief decides to slam the door to this camp on me. He is clearly *Sabuknu* here and it would only take one command to shut me out.

Sweet Berry is found, alive and well! I am standing only a few yards away from her as I speak. She is sitting on the floor by the edge of her shelter and I can make out the faint birthmark on her forehead. She appears to be a perfectly formed little nine-year-old, but deceptively small for her age. She strikes me as bright and full of life. With her is a five-year-old boy whom she appears to be instructing about the palming language. It's quite fascinating to watch her. Right now she has put a clay cup in the boy's hands. She's letting him turn it over and become familiar with it. Now she's tracing signs on the boy's palm, signs that no doubt stand for the object in his hand. That's exactly what I must have her do for me.

Also in the shelter is an older woman, no more than fifty but the oldest of any of the women I've seen here. Possibly she's the matriarch of the community. Something about her suggests the schoolmarm. In fact, this particular guild must be the tribe's school, or at least one of them, for she too has a child with her, a little girl of six or seven, and she's doing the same thing. She has just put a piece of fruit in the girl's hand and is palming the sign for it.

It's absolutely gripping to watch this. This is a language the *Jakareme* had to invent on their own, word by word over many generations—a language without antecedents of any kind, fashioned entirely from the raw need to communicate, from drives wired in the brain. But is that possible? Can language spring up spontaneously, like wild flowers? I've always understood it takes language to beget language. Even wild flowers have to have seeds. So how in the world did they manage this? The linguistic world will be spellbound when they learn about it. And they will learn of it if I do my job right.

For the remainder of this afternoon I intend to stay right here at the side of Sweet Berry's shelter and take notes. I'm not close enough to catch much of the palming, but I'll pick up what I can. Observing her, this little tyke seems quite sure of herself. She's pure pleasure to watch and must be gifted to have teaching responsibility at her age. She will instruct me too, if the chief doesn't block it. I'm not even supposed to be here on the women's side.

CHAPTER ELEVEN

ENCOUNTERS WITH SWEET BERRY

DAY FOUR
(no entry)

THE MORNING OF DAY FIVE

SO MUCH HAPPENED YESTERDAY I was in no frame of mind to record a thing, not even last evening when I got back to camp. It's now early morning of the fifth day and I'm still here in my campsite trying to puzzle out what to do next. In a word, things did not go well yesterday, not at all, although it ended on a better note. But let me record events in order of their happening.

First thing yesterday morning I planned to make contact with the chief. During the night I had the idea of presenting to him the leopard skin that *Sabuknu* gave me as *Teeku-mi* and I took our leave. He had taken it from the pile of skins that made up his throne. An animal skin like this would make an ideal cushion for this local *Sabuknu*. It's quite luxurious and ought to soften him up. That was my intention but as it turned out I could not present it to him. When I approached his compound early yesterday morning a conclave was in progress of seemingly all the males in the camp, all lined up in the courtyard. The chief was standing before them, palming his young lieutenant, Charlie-Two, who quickly passed it on to one of the other underlings who repeated it and so on down the lines. It was a slow, lugubrious process, if you can imagine it, like signals going over telephone lines at the pace of a caterpillar. The chief could be half finished before the end of the line got his opening words. I had no idea what the call-up was about but was afraid it had to do with the alien. What happened later more or less confirmed this. The chief is clearly unsettled about my presence here.

There was no sense in carrying the leopard skin around in the heat of the day, so I ventured up into the bamboo grove that surrounded the chief's compound and slung it over a branch, high enough to be out of the way, awaiting a more propitious time.

I then went on directly to Sweet Berry's shelter. I gave no thought to announcing my presence and actually entering. It's taboo and I was not about to have them hold this against me as well. And the matriarch living in the shelter with Sweet Berry was not one to be messed with. I've dubbed her Dragon Lady. No doubt she knows all about the alien. I can't afford to have the camp's matriarch turn against me also.

But first, let me describe this particular little school guild in more detail. The shelter has four residents— Dragon Lady, Sweet Berry, and the two children. To keep them from straying off, each child is vine-tethered to one of the tree trunks that supports the shelter's roof covering. Luckily for me, Sweet Berry herself has a little spot on the bamboo floor right near the edge of the enclosure. As I've mentioned, none of these shelters have walls, just a single vine line for sidings tied to bamboo trunks, and so, as it happened, I was able to get close to Sweet Berry from outside without having to give myself away. The little birth mark on her forehead that accounts for her name—*Lunas-nili*—was quite visible close up like this. From where she sat, I could actually reach out and touch her, but not without frightening the poor girl to death. But the other night I thought of a way to make contact with her and yesterday it worked like a charm.

Along one edge of the pond by my campsite there's an abundance of pink water lilies with quite a lovely fragrance. So first thing yesterday morning I picked a few and brought them with me. When I arrived at Sweet Berry's shelter, she was sitting at her usual spot by the flooring's edge. She was alone, fussing with her foot which seemed to be troubling her. Dragon Lady was doing something with the two children. From my perch at the edge of the shelter, I reached in and lightly brushed a water lily across Sweet Berry's pretty little face. This of course got her attention. Then I dropped the lily in her hand. As I said, she was alone, not with any of the children, and what she did next was rather startling. She reached for the tether of the five-year-old boy and tugged it. The boy crawled over to her and she took his hand and placed the lily in it. She waited patiently as he felt what it was with both of his hands. Then she took his hand and began palming. Next she drew the hand holding the flower up to the child's nose and again began palming. I found her behavior most remarkable. I had sprung a little surprise on her and she immediately turned it into a teaching opportunity. After a while the kid crawled away, and Sweet Berry sat alone, passing the flower back and forth beneath her delicate tiny nostrils.

Then I dropped a second one in her lap and she picked it up with one hand and with the other reached out about her in that sweeping way. I brushed a third lily across her face. She reached for it and encountered my hand. She drew back instinctively, but then stopped. She is a very intelligent little girl, that's quite obvious, for she grasped at once that these were gifts. I brushed the flower along her cheek once again and this time she took my hand and held it, tentatively at first, and then more relaxed.

She's a curious little tyke for she immediately discovered *Teeku's* ring. I took her hand and drew my four fingers across her palm, twice in rapid succession, followed by two taps. She returned the greeting. I assume she knew it was a man's hand, but I can't be sure as she may never have felt a grown male hand before. At once she reached for my identity string and again drew back when she felt the relic pouch. I palmed the *it's OK* sign several times on her wrist. Again she reached for the relic, for *Odilia sannu*. To play the game, I too reached for her identity string as well, but she must have already sensed that I am very different than anyone she's ever known before. It's interesting. The *Jakareme* don't know they are beset by these sense privations. How would they? How could they know what they lack? But Sweet Berry seemed aware that I was different, like my knowing she was there without first having to feel for her. She seemed not the least bit confounded by this. I found her reactions rather curious actually.

All of this took place with the Dragon Lady only a few feet away, happily without any awareness of my presence. Suddenly she moved toward us, felt for Sweet Berry's swaying, outstretched hand and began palming her. I gathered she was informing Sweet Berry that the two of them were to take their charges out on the trail—quite possibly for trail orientation. I say this because Sweet Berry drew the Dragon Lady's attention to her foot, and the Dragon Lady left without her young partner, tethering the two children to herself.

I seized the occasion to join Sweet Berry on the flooring and took a good look at her foot. She did not seem surprised or frightened at this. It turned out that she had a deep splinter on the sole of her right foot. The splinter was nasty and part of it had broken off fairly deep under the skin; I would have to make an incision to get at it. (Since the episode with Damian-Two, I carry my medical bag as a matter of course now.) I bathed the foot in iodine and tried to reassure her with the single-finger *OK sign* across her inner wrist that the pain would be brief. I think somehow she understood.

I was in the middle of this procedure when disaster struck: Dragon Lady burst into the shelter all agitated with only the seven-year-old girl in tow. The boy was nowhere in sight. She had not tapped her code on entering, and her heavy steps caused Sweet Berry to stiffen and jerk back. The Dragon Lady may have thought the boy had returned on his own. (As I pieced things together later, it seems he slipped away from her when they were out on the trail.) She rushed toward Sweet Berry with arms swinging wildly. I jumped up at once but could not avoid her crashing right into me. She grasped at once that I was a large male intruder who had violated the great taboo, and had to be the alien. Immediately she flew back out onto the trail and, dragging the seven-year old behind her, groped her way upstream towards the chief's dwelling.

Sweet Berry certainly felt the Dragon Lady's agitation and sudden, abrupt departure, but she had no idea why this was happening, that the boy was missing, and probably no real appreciation for the great taboo and that its violation would outrage her elder this way. I foresaw the trouble coming but had no choice but to finish up with Sweet Berry's foot. I worked quickly and was just completing the bandaging when the chief's four underlings came up from the main trail, the pole points of the two in front swaying out before them. The chief's main sidekick, the one I call Charlie-Two, was in the lead and was clearly looking for trouble. The four let the Dragon Lady come into the shelter from behind them but they themselves did not enter. The Dragon Lady advanced towards Sweet Berry, arms swinging away. Naturally by this time I had stepped just outside. In an instant the Dragon Lady was upon Sweet Berry. From where I stood I could see Sweet Berry draw her elder's hand to the bandaging on her foot and the two began palming.

Meanwhile, the underlings were circling the shelter, looking for me. The sides of these shelters, as I said, consist merely of a single vine line, like a railing, and this they used as guide as they made their way around, swinging their poles out in wide sweeps. It could not occur to them that anyone would move any distance from this or any other life line, so all I had to do was stay a few yards away to persuade them no one was there any longer.

One of the vine lines led from behind the shelter deeper into the bamboo grove and Charlie-Two and another of the underlings followed it. I could not tell where this vine path led but I suspect it too winds up at the mysterious cave in the bluff up behind the chief's shelter. If I am right, this particular shelter seems to be the only other dwelling besides the chief's with a vine path up to that cave. Whatever the significance of the cave, this fact might be a sign of the Dragon Lady's standing in the camp. And Sweet Berry too, as her underling. As for the cave, this is terra incognita I have yet to look into.

The other two underlings who remained behind, after again making their rounds and finding no one, tapped and drew the Dragon Lady to the edge of the shelter. She was still agitated and seemed not at all mollified by Sweet Berry's bandaged foot. I suspect the Dragon Lady was telling them the taboo violation and the boy's disappearance were connected. I was fairly certain I would have no trouble finding the boy so I went onto the main trail in the direction the Dragon Lady had gone off in earlier with the two children. It wasn't long before I spotted him, splashing in the brook, enjoying himself like any five-year-old with no inkling of the trouble he was causing. I went down into the water and took him by the hand—he came along quite willingly—and led him back up to the trail.

That was when I realized how quickly the mood in the camp had changed. Seemingly almost every male in the place was about with poles swinging away, pointed end out. I took the boy back to his shelter, keeping to the grass outside the vine lines to avoid the traffic. When we got there, the underlings had left and the Dragon Lady and Sweet Berry were engrossed in palming. I tapped my signature on the flooring and both occupants froze. Then, after a moment, Sweet Berry tapped back and came forward, swaying her hand before her. The Dragon Lady stayed where she was and took up her pole. Soon as we made contact, I took Sweet Berry's hand and placed it on the boy's head. The effect was instantaneous. Sweet Berry leaned over and felt the boy's face, then embraced him. She felt back for her elder and taking her hand drew it to the boy. The elder's relief was palpable too, but in the palming that ensued, as I stood there watching, I sensed the Dragon Lady was convinced I had been responsible for the boy's disappearance. How could I have found the boy and brought him back if I did not have him under my control all along? By now I believe Sweet Berry knew better, and from what I could see, there was considerable back and forth between them about this.

There was little more I could do to help the situation so I tapped my departure (five rapid strokes on the flooring) and went back down on the trail, heading upstream. When I got to the chief's shelter I saw that no one was there, precisely the chance I had been hoping for. I went up to the grove, got the leopard skin I had hung there earlier and went into the enclosure. There was a woven, mat-like cloth covering the place where this local *Sabuknu* normally sat, something that must had been fashioned for him as a throne seat. I placed the animal skin over it. The chief would have to know the alien had done this, and hopefully it would make points for me. I must have time now with Sweet Berry to learn this palm language but won't stand a chance without his backing.

In the next moment I saw the chief feeling his way along the path that leads down from the cave. His protégé sidekick Charlie-Two was right behind. I stepped off the flooring and watched them as they entered the shelter. The chief discovered the leopard skin right away. He picked it up and turned it over and over in his hands, feeling its fur. But to my surprise he then set it aside. Nor did he indicate anything about it to Charlie-Two. The chief was surely aware how it got there, but he was not about to accept anything from this intruder. Understandable enough. He could not yet have gotten the report about the boy being found or about my ministrations on Sweet Berry's foot, so my presence in the camp still has to be a huge threat to him.

I went back on the trail. The men of the community were out everywhere in full force, so I went upstream to the crossover point, waded across and made my way back down to my campsite.

In all, yesterday was a frustrating day. I was very grateful to be back in my camp last evening, alone with my thoughts. I hope today will turn out to be better.

BACK AT MY CAMP AT THE END OF DAY FIVE

Let me record today's events which, I'm relieved to report, did go better than yesterday at least.

This morning I knew I simply had to get through to the chief today. I don't have many days left here. I figured by now he will have learned that I took care of Sweet Berry's foot and that I found the boy. Unless of course the

Dragon Lady has poisoned his mind. She was bound to wonder how I could bring the boy back like that if I hadn't taken him away in the first place. But little Sweet Berry knows better, and it's just possible that her view of me will prevail. She strikes me as a little fighter with her own take on things. Anyway, I would know in short order. I was determined to get somewhere with this fellow today. I took along the two other gifts that *Teeku-mi* brought up, the sheath knife and the clay water pitcher. And some more of these fragrant water lilies, this time for old Dragon Lady herself.

Once on the main trail heading for the chief's shelter, I could tell that things already were different. None of the men I passed on the trail had their spear ends pointed out. I went first to the shelter of Damian-Two and his protégé, Carlito-Two, to test the waters.

It went well. I tapped my identity code on the flooring of their shelter and Damian-Two responded right away. They greeted me without hesitation, virtually with open arms. I checked Carlito-Two's arm and his mentor's legs, and both are doing just fine. I didn't stay long but everything seemed quite normal and uncomplicated.

Then I headed up the path to the chief's shelter, but he was not there. Neither was his side-kick, Charlie-Two, nor the other underlings. Nor did I see the animal skin I left here for him yesterday afternoon.

So I went downstream to Sweet Berry's shelter to see her, and also the Dragon Lady for I had something in mind about her. Amazingly things went better with this tough bird. When I arrived at the shelter and tapped my code on the flooring, I could see the Dragon Lady freeze. But Sweet Berry tapped right back and came forward, swaying her little arm. We made contact and felt for each other's identity strings. She especially lingered over my relic which seems to fascinate her. And the smooth material of my shirt and of course *Teeku's* ring too all came in for inspection. These are the things that make up what I look like to her, and for this bright little nine year old it's all wondrously new.

Sweet Berry reached back to the Dragon Lady and drew her to where I was standing at the shelter's edge. Perhaps more by instinct than anything else, the Dragon Lady extended her palm and I drew the greeting across it with my finger tips. After a flicker of hesitation, she did the same. We felt each other's identity strings and she too experienced the relic for the first time. Then the other things too, the unexpected shirt (as I mentioned, the men here are all naked to the waist), and *Teeku's* ring which seems to intrigue everyone. I deftly placed a water lily in her hand and did the same for Sweet Berry. Sweet Berry instantly drew it to her nose. And the Dragon Lady too, before long, had the flower up against her face. Even here on *dundi lano,* when a gentleman calls on a lady, flowers go a long way.

Next I placed the clay pitcher in the Dragon Lady's hand. Artifacts from the world below the mountain were not uncommon, but apparently nothing like this. Her hands explored the unfamiliar object and before long she knew she had been given something of real utility. Abruptly she patted the palm of her hand against mine twice, which I took to mean thanks. It was done rather quickly but I felt it was sincere. In the next instant she withdrew, leaving me alone at the shelter's edge with her young partner.

I had Sweet Berry sit down so I could examine her foot. I changed the dressing and drew a single finger twice across her inner wrist signally *OK, good*. She palmed back something I could not decipher. But I'm learning. From what I gather so far, *Yes* is expressed by the rapid sweep of one fingernail across the palm. *No* by rapid back and forth sweeps of the fingernails across the back of the hand. *I don't know* is expressed by briefly playing four fingers on the palm as on a keyboard instrument.

I brought Sweet Berry's hand to her foot, and then to my palm, trusting her pedagogical intelligence would catch what I was after. It worked. She palmed me the sign for *foot*—a single finger drawn across the palm terminated with five very rapid dots (doubtless representing the toes). Using this method, I learned the signs for *hand*—two inside fingertips drawn across the palm, with five rapid dots. The sign for *head* is a circle with one fingertip, with a smaller circle inside, probably standing for the mouth.

Sweet Berry understood my intent and brought various objects to me at the edge of the enclosure. I learned that a bowl was a circle drawn on the palm twice with a fingernail. A big bowl was the same thing drawn three times. The *Jakareme* palm signs have the quality of simple ideographs, like drawing a square for an enclosure. These signs are further embellished by touching specific places on the palm, wrist, or on one or more of the fingers, knuckles, or even on the arm or chest. The way you touch too is important, with palm or one or more fingertips or fingernails. There are other elements also, like sweeps of the fingertips or of the nails down or across the palm or on the back of the hand, or rolling the knuckles or the fist. And then there are the coded tappings. The *Jakareme* couldn't possibly have evolved an alphabet, but the tappings bear a loose resemblance to Morse Code where dashes and dots are expressed by the interval of time the finger rests on the palm, rather than by tone length. They must use this code scheme for notions and entities that are not easily spelled out graphically. I would give anything to know the code for the chief, but at this point don't even yet know how to ask for it. Very likely it's the same code as that used for the floor tappings. For him, it's three strong, slowly executed taps.

Before long, the Dragon Lady came up to Sweet Berry and sought to draw her back into their regular routine. Interestingly, Sweet Berry did not let her—the little private school she and I had going was still in session. I pointed to her chest and repeated the code she tapped on the flooring. In her case: one short, two long, one short, two long, followed by three rapid taps. She came back with the sweep of one finger across my palm saying, *Yes, that's me.* So at least now I know how to identify her to the chief.

The two children were becoming restless. They had no idea what was going on a few feet from them. I could see that the Dragon Lady was growing impatient too so I left, but not before giving both Sweet Berry and her schoolmarm mentor the *Jakareme* parting sign, four fingertips swept slowly across the palm three times followed by a single tap. They palmed me back, Sweet Berry eagerly and warmly, the Dragon Lady more coolly.

I went back on the trail resolved to establish contact with the chief. I had brought along *Teeku-mi's* sheath knife thinking it might be just the thing to break the ice with his royal highness. Luckily I found the chief in his shelter, along with Charlie-Two. They knew instantly who it was who tapped on the flooring. Both bodies stiffened but Charlie-Two answered back right away and as I entered, both the chief and he stood up. Charlie-Two moved forward, swaying his hand and we contacted and went through the usual greeting rituals. This youth had never touched me before but he knew all the marks. His fingers quickly felt for the relic pouch, *Teeku's* ring, the shirt and the beard. After this he turned and palmed the chief but did not hand me over to him. The chief for his part kept himself back. I wasn't going to stand for that so I reached out to palm the chief's hand. He withdrew it abruptly. I reached over and thrust the sheath knife into his hand before he had time to react. He had no difficulty recognizing what it was. He took the knife out of the sheath, felt its fine point, and then handed it over to his underling. Charlie-Two examined it in the same meticulous way. They began palming and what happened next told me I had made zero progress. Charlie-Two restored the knife to its sheath and stuck it in his own vine belt while the chief turned his back and withdrew to the edge of the shelter. Charlie-Two reached for my hand and palmed it with the end of his fist, striking it forcibly three times, a gesture I took to mean that I was to leave. The meeting was over. Also, each had taken up his pole. I had little choice but to comply, which I did with the appropriate signal. Soon as they sensed my steps leaving the flooring, they began palming again. I stayed nearby, watching them.

It wasn't long before the chief and his sidekick took off up the path to the cave behind their grove. I followed for a while but saw that the other three underlings were already stationed at its entrance. It's something of a mystery what could be drawing them up there. But any exploration of the cave will have to wait 'til tomorrow.

For the rest of the afternoon I explored some of the camp's outer trails to see where they led. There are many such trails, spread out like a network all over this side of the mountain. Then I came back to my campsite for a bath in the pond and an evening meal, still pondering how to win the chief over. My time here is running out.

CHAPTER TWELVE

THE CAVE REVEALS ITS SECRET

DAY SIX
RECORDED AT THE END OF
A BREAKTHROUGH DAY

I SET OUT EARLY THIS MORNING and when I got to the brook's crossover and was preparing to wade across, scores of *Jakareme* males suddenly appeared on the far side. For all their silence they seemed agitated and in a huge rush. In short order they began splashing across the water towards me, slipping and sliding on the rock slime. Fortunately each man was connected by waist lines to the one directly behind; when someone fell the ones behind would instantly pull him back up on his feet. At the head of this urgent, ragged line were two of the chief's underlings, poles probing the water as they hurried the pack across. Once everyone was over I took up the rear.

The two eventually led us off the main trail down a branch path, and then after a while down yet another branch and then still another. This last path was new and had been hardly used; its vine line looked like it had just been strung out. We followed the vine until we were fairly deep into the jungle, surrounded by dense undergrowth.

As we made our way, I spotted the fleeting movement of a good-sized animal not far back in from the trail. Taking no chances I took out my gun.

The procession suddenly came to a halt. We had come to the end of the vine line in the heart of dense jungle thicket. There standing ahead of us was the third underling, swaying his pole as the vine line's movement announced our presence to him. He and the two underlings made contact and began furiously palming away. Their youngest member, Charlie-Two, was nowhere in sight.

What I surmised—which turned out to be the case— was that the four underlings had been setting up vine lines for a new trail and that, somehow, Charlie-Two had gotten separated from the other three. One of the underlings had stayed behind while the other two rushed back to camp for reinforcements. It's not hard to imagine the cause of their alarm. What could be more terrorizing for a *Jakareme* than to be out on the trail and to lose contact with the vine line and the others you are with? How do you recover? Which way do you turn? You could be standing only a yard or two away from the others and still be fatally cut off, fatally alone.

On a signal, the line of natives began to move out into the underbrush, each man probing the ground or swinging his pole to one side or the other. This rescue line, anchored to the trail, methodically swept through the undergrowth like the seconds hand of a clock. What I was witnessing must be standard practice for this kind of crisis.

I went ahead, keeping well clear of them. The brush was dense so it was not easy to see more than a few yards ahead. Jungle birds were screeching about something, perhaps about our intrusion. Or were they warning each other about a jungle cat? The scene felt ominous to me. I had my gun ready and it is very lucky that I did. I was already some distance into the thicket when I almost stumbled upon Charlie-Two. He was crouched on the jungle floor with his head in his hands, looking disoriented and very lost. And just yards away, studying him, hunched a sleek black panther. On catching sight of me the cat turned to slink away but, taking no chances, I shot him on the spot. Charlie-Two must have felt air reverberations or perhaps the movement in the grassy undergrowth, for he jumped up and swung his pole wildly about him. In the process he moved a few feet and almost tripped over the panther's warm dead body. All this happened just as the rescue line came and collided into him. They made a great fuss over finding him, the chief's favorite, and doubly so when one by one they discovered the animal's warm body at his feet. As far as they knew, the chief's protégé killed the animal himself, single-handedly.

What Charlie-Two did next rather stunned me and made me appreciate the stuff he is made of. He poked at the others to step back. Then he took out his knife, the very knife I had tried giving the chief yesterday, and set about skinning the animal. I jumped in to work with him at the other end. Charlie-Two is a smart fellow and he quickly figured out who was helping him and what had happened. He reached for my hand and patted my palm several times strongly, one of the *Jakareme* signs for gratitude. The others had no idea I was there and I was careful not to give my presence away. They all stood there patiently as we worked, fully mindful I imagine that the underling, whatever he was up to, was next in line to become their chief and his wishes had to be obeyed.

An hour later the procession made its way back to camp, this time in triumph with Charlie-Two at the head, the bloody, black panther skin slung across his shoulders. The procession turned into the chief's courtyard and waited while the underlings tapped their identity one by one and entered the shelter, keeping to its edge. The chief stood up and came forward, waiting expectantly, arms still quiet at his side. Charlie-Two tapped last and when the chief understood that his young protégé had been found, his swaying arms thrust out in unabashed joy. It was a delight to witness. None of the others could see this, of course, but all could imagine the chief's pleasure. The two of them palmed away, and Charlie-Two very shortly made a presentation of the animal skin to his chief. This too had to be explained with more palming. Before long all four underlings were in conversation in this manner, and word was being passed down the line to the others. The favorite had been lost and was found. The joy of the occasion was palpable but it was all in the motion of their hands and bodies; their faces were mostly blank, as expressionless as ever.

I did not linger at the site. This was no place for me now. I felt confident Charlie-Two would duly inform the chief of the alien's part in the morning's events and my chances with the chief would have to improve. But even so I had to give this time.

I went back on the trail and made my way downstream to Sweet Berry. I planned to go up to the side of the shelter and watch Sweet Berry do her teaching and hopefully gain further intelligence about the language. But when I got there Sweet Berry was gone. Dragon Lady was there, busy with the two children, but Sweet Berry's spot was empty. But something at her place caught my eye, and I confess it absolutely startled me. There on the flooring where the girl normally kept herself was a neatly folded purple cloth. I went to the edge of the flooring and leaned in and got hold of it. It was a finely made purple scarf, too fine for anything the *Jakareme* could have fashioned. It looked very much in fact like the purple scarves and sashes *Jakareme* mothers wore in the *Chiroki* village. I thought of that group of grim native women peering at us as *Teeku-mi* and I set out for *dundi lano* a week ago, all wearing a strip of deep purple cloth like this. The *masi-Jakareme*, *Teeku-mi* called them, *bearers of cursed children.* But how on earth did Sweet Berry come upon such a thing? Was it her mother's? How did this cloth suddenly show up like this? Seeing this purple scarf was unsettling, I must say, like a goad, reminding me why this little girl's father brought me to *dundi lano* in the first place.

It was at this point that I thought about the cave. I had nothing better to do. Now was as good a time as any to explore it. I hadn't brought my flashlight with me so I went back upstream past the chief's shelter up to the fording spot and back down on the other side to my campsite. I also retrieved the medical kit I neglected to take with me when I started out earlier, which was fortunate as I soon found a good use for it.

Coming back down the main trail of the settlement, I got to the chief's quarters. The courtyard was now empty but he was there in the shelter with his underlings, still in hand-conversation with his Charlie-Two, getting I hope the full story. I had no intention of interrupting this. I slipped up behind the shelter and traced the vine line through the grove up to the cave. No one was guarding the entrance. I switched on the flashlight and went in.

I had not gone more than five steps when I caught Sweet Berry in the light beam. She was kneeling over what seemed to be an adult woman stretched out on the cave floor. She was wiping the woman's forehead with a cloth. As I shined the beam on the woman's face it surprised me that she abruptly turned her head away. I couldn't imagine she had seen the light, no more than Sweet Berry, but by instinct I turned off my light. As it was, the cave is fairly shallow and the daylight seeping in from outside was enough for what I needed to see.

I moved in closer. The woman's eyes were shut. She was about forty, overly thin, garbed in that crudely made garment worn by the *Jakareme* women. And she was obviously quite ill. The nine-year-old Sweet Berry was bathing her face and neck, doing this with unusual tenderness I thought. As my vision adjusted to the dim light, I noticed that the cloth she was using for this purpose was purple and had to be another one of these *masi-Jakareme* sashes, like the one in her shelter. Curious, I glanced around the cave. Spread out along natural ledges in the cave wall were a series of dark objects. Putting my light on them I spotted clay cups and bowls, quite a few of them, many of them broken. And then, in the far corner of the cave, my light fell upon a quantity of these very same purple sashes all neatly folded. There must have been a score or more of them.

Sweet Berry finished what she came to do. She palmed

something to the woman who barely responded, then she got up and left. I moved in to take her place but in the poor light I kicked against something—what turned out to be the water pitcher I had given Dragon Lady the day before. Luckily I was able to right it before spilling its contents, for I would soon be needing water. But, typical of me, my clumsiness provoked a loud oath. The woman stirred at this. When I played the light on her face, I found her staring up at me. Whoever she was, she was no *Jakareme*.

"*La Chiroki?*" I said to her (*are you Chiroki?*)

She did not answer at first. I think she was terribly frightened. She had never seen artificial light before. And my beard and skin color were utterly strange to her.

I extinguished the light and repeated the question, and finally she answered weakly, "*La*" (*Yes*).

I thought of the purple sashes in the corner of the cave. "*La masi-Jakareme?*" I asked (*are you the bearer of a child of the curse?*)

After a pause again a weak, "*La.*"

I hadn't any doubt this was Sweet Berry's mother, *Teeku-mi's* wife. From what I remembered, she disappeared shortly after the daughter was taken to *dundi lano*, nine years ago.

Teeku-mi had mentioned his wife's name the night we camped on our way up the mountain. "*La Tolani?*" I asked, "*Kinasi na Lunas-nili?*" (*Are you Tolani, Sweet Berry's mother?*)

The woman's eyes went shut and she turned her head away, but I had hit home.

I took her hand and drew it to my chest. *"Chilani-no chilani na Teeku-mi,"* I said (*friend-here is a friend of Teeku-mi*).

She turned back wide-eyed at this and she made an effort to raise herself, but lacked the strength. She just lay there staring. I could see her eyes taking in the hair on my face, the clothing on my upper body, the light skin. Instinctively she stretched out a feeble arm for my identity string and jerked back when she felt the relic. Again her eyes fell shut. All this was too much for her.

She was clearly feverish. Her hand was burning hot, as was her brow when I felt it. I had already seen enough yellow in the whites of her eyes to recognize the signs. She was malarial, a diagnosis confirmed in the next instant when she began shaking. There was an animal skin lying by her side and I drew it over her. (By now it came as no real surprise to find it was the leopard skin I'd carried up the mountain and given to the chief only yesterday.)

Fortunately I had an effective anti-malarial drug in my kit that kills these parasites in fairly short order. With luck she should be out of danger in a few days, just the interval of time I have left. At least what I began today will save her life.

I poured water into a clay cup, and raising her up had her swallow one of these pills (*chloroquine phosphate*). She seemed perplexed at this but offered no resistance. In eight hours I'll have to do this again, and then two more times each day for the next two days.

What she needed after that was rest. After making sure there was water for her, I told her *goodbye,* first in *Chiroki* and then in *Jakareme* palm-talk, sweeping four fingertips slowly across the palm three times, followed by a single tap. A faint smile on her lips reassured me. Whatever she took me for, she was not rejecting me.

I had barely stood up when I heard sounds at the entrance. There, silhouetted in the doorway was the tall, gaunt figure of the chief. In the next instant he tapped his code—three strong, rhythmic strokes struck on the floor of the cave. Weak as she was, the woman took a stone at her side and tapped back. I stepped out of the way as he moved forward, carefully feeling ahead for her with his pole. I saw her glance over at me uneasily as she waited for him.

The chief sat by her and they briefly palmed. Then they just sat there in *Jakareme* silence, the chief holding her hand in both of his. From time to time, like Sweet Berry, he would stroke her forehead. Sometimes when he did this she would stare at me. The incongruity of it all really struck me—the chief in his sightless world trying to comfort her, and we, the woman and I, sharing another world entirely, one he had not the slightest inkling of. I can imagine the shock my presence was causing her. For nine years she had been living in the world of sight all by herself. And over time, in her actual day-to-day living, this *Jakareme* world of sightless silence became hers as well. It had to be that way. My presence crashed through that, rudely, like a loud, unexpected thunder clap from out of nowhere. After a while as we sat there, she looked over at me, and sick as she was, her face brightened. She smiled, and for a fleeting moment I glimpsed where her daughter's perfect loveliness came from. Then she closed her eyes and dozed off.

Perhaps I should have left but I could not bring myself to go. I sat there, watching the woman drift in and

The explorer administers a drug to the malarial woman in the cave.

out of sleep, observing the chief as he sat by her side, never letting go of her hand. This went on for what seemed like an hour or more. *Jakareme* time is like that, just drifting along, without clocks, without hurry. I was glad for the time, for I had a lot to sort through myself.

Before me was a sighted woman hidden away in a cave filled with pottery and purple scarves, obviously held by the chief as someone very special and personally dear to him. Most likely, over the years that she has been here, this woman, *Tolani*, has done many good things for the community. But I greatly suspect she kept herself separate, isolated in this cave. Except for her daughter, and the chief and his underlings who I imagine bring her meals, and maybe the Dragon Lady, I doubt the rest of the community knows anything about her. That's my guess anyhow. It's easy enough for someone with sight to be present here and remain hidden, to know everyone and everything and yet stay unknown.

There've been others before her, over the generations, the mothers, the *masi-Jakareme* who made their way here, who would not just give up their child to *dundi lano* and its evil spirits, remarkable women who must have been like silent angels to the community taking shape on this mountain. How else were the *Jakareme* able to select this perfect site by the brook? How else could they manage to set up a well-ordered camp, learn to feed and clothe themselves? The pile of neatly folded, purple sashes in the cover of this cave told the story, a tragic yet marvelously noble tale, one almost beyond imagining.

Then once, when this woman's eyes opened and she looked over at me, I saw my chance and I broke the silence.

"*Tolani*," I said in my halting *Chiroki,* pointing to the chief, "*Chilani-no soto fulana sabuknu-ni.*" (*I want meet this sabuknu*).

The woman stared at me with heavy eyes, eyes that would have been so lovely were it not for the disease and discoloration. But she said nothing.

I switched on my light and played it on the chief sitting by her. I repeated my request. "*Soto fulana sabuknu-ni. Jinji Tolani pomago chilani-no, ladi?*" (*I want to meet this chief. Please you help me, ok?*).

She rather frowned at this, but after a long hesitation said in a voice barely audible, "*La, dono asum?*" (*All right, but how?*).

(*I'll translate our conversation here, rather than record the* Chiroki.)

"Tell chief you have friend here," I said. "Friend good. Tell him friend want meet chief."

Tolani withdrew her hand from the chief and began palming him. After a few moments of this the chief's body stiffened.

"Chief want know who?" she said.

"Tell chief is friend who gave animal skin," I said.

She palmed this and the chief's jaw hardened.

"Tell chief friend has new gift," I said.

She did this and then said weakly, "Chief not want gift."

"Tell chief friend want meet," I said again. "Tell chief," I repeated.

As she relayed this message, I took a rock and struck my code on the cave floor, letting the chief physically sense my presence. Then I went ahead and swept four fingers across his palm, twice in rapid succession, followed by two taps with the knuckle—the traditional *Jakareme* greeting, and I reached for his identity string. He seemed startled at my abruptness but when I placed my palm up against his, he returned the gesture, and then, after a moment, he felt for the expected, strange object dangling from my neck. He knew all about me of course and I think curiosity undid his reserve. He reached to feel my beard too, and my shirt. Then his hand went back to the band of metal on my finger, lingering over it briefly with his own fingers. That gave me an idea.

I took the chief's hand and before he could react, I slipped my ring over his finger. Luckily it proved an easy fit. The chief was taken aback of course. He kept touching the object on his finger then he reached for my hand and felt for the ring no longer there. Another long pause, as his dignity absorbed all this, then very slowly he stretched out for my hand and taking it in both of his, he squeezed, not very warmly, but even so I knew it was a *Jakareme* gesture of appreciation. I was getting somewhere.

I turned to *Tolani*, who for all her misery looked pleased at what she had just witnessed. "How say *'young helper'* in *Jakareme*?" I asked, extending my hand.

She thought about that for a moment, then traced the sign, and I in turn took his hand and asked, *"Young helper is OK?"* (I had already learned from Sweet Berry that *OK* is expressed by running a single finger twice across the inside wrist.)

The chief understood my meaning. He repeated the sign for *OK,* and then circled the end of his fist twice on my palm, another *Jakareme* way I figure to express gratitude. And another step forward.

I did not have the sense he wished for more conversation. And *Tolani* was tiring and once again began to shake. I covered her with the leopard skin and after a bit she dozed off. I reached for the chief's hands and gave the *Jakareme* goodbye sign (three slow sweeps of the fingertips across the palm followed by a single tap). As I moved to go, *Tolani* opened her eyes. "I come back" I said. She peered at me for a moment, as if only half comprehending, and then a lovely, faint smile spread across the pallor of her lips.

It is early evening and I am back at my campsite, frying some fish for a tired, thoroughly famished anthropological linguist. It goes without saying this has been a breakthrough day for my enterprise here on *dundi lano*. With *Tolani* in the picture, even sick as she is, I have the perfect instructor for this silent language, this language that so intrigued first Fr. Christopher Damian and then me, drawing both of us up a dangerous river in its pursuit. Now with this woman I'll glean more in an hour than I could ever get from little Sweet Berry, much as she is willing.

I learned some interesting things from *Tolani* late this afternoon when I went back to the cave with her medication. She was asleep when I got there, but already she seemed a bit less feverish. And she must have done a lot of thinking in the meanwhile because when she opened her eyes and saw me, she brightened and reached for my hand. I must say she has a truly inviting smile, weak as she is. After giving her the anti-malarial pill and some fresh water that I had brought up from the brook, I asked if we could talk. She nodded. In my meager *Chiroki*, I told her she spoke the *Jakareme* hand language very well. She seemed amused at this, probably more at my *Chiroki* which had to sound unnatural to her, even if she had not heard it spoken in years, or spoken it herself. No matter, she understood me. I asked her how long it took for her to learn the *Jakareme* language. She smiled at this and said, *"bulgani, bulgani (very long time)."*

Then I asked her something that had been on my mind for days. "How say 'father' in hand language?" I said, stretching my palm out to her.

She looked strangely at me for a moment, then uttered in a voice I could barely hear, *"Jakareme* not have language for father."

It was as I thought. "Also not for 'mother'?" I asked.

Tolani stared at me but said nothing.

It makes sense the *Jakareme* would have no word for *father*. There were no fathers here, and if anything the great taboo is designed to insure it stays that way. But if the taboo was set up for that purpose, someone must have understood what fathers are for. Who but these purple-clad *Chiroki* mothers, the *masi-Jakareme*? How could the *Jakareme* themselves have any notion of fatherhood? That there is such a thing as begetting a child. It's fascinating to think that here we have a tribe that understands nothing at all about parenting, that does not even have a word for it. If there are no fathers, no birth mothers, there are no brothers and sisters, there are no families. Everyone here has been dropped off as a baby from outside, delivered as if by storks. Except for

Sweet Berry. She has her mother. But does Sweet Berry understand who this woman really is, that she is her *birth* mother? Does the *Jakareme* palm language allow for such notions? And what of her father? If I could get *Teeku-mi* to come here, would this little girl ever understand who he is to her?

Now as I sit here by the fire in the dusk, I'm still thinking about this language and how impoverished it must be. There are scores of *Jakareme* just a short hike upstream, but they have no words for what I see and hear right now—the last streaks of daylight sinking in the evening sky, the distant screech of what must be a huge bird circling its nest for the night, and just a moment ago the rustle of some small animal nearby in the underbrush, drawn I suppose by the fire and the smell of frying fish. There's been rain this afternoon too, higher up in the mountain, and the fresh current is stirring the water lilies on my side of the pond. The *Jakareme* know nothing of any of this. There's a kind of enchantment on this mountain at night, but what does *night* itself mean to them? Just the advent of welcomed coolness, probably. Do they have a word for daylight, for darkness, for this perfect stillness? Not likely. But I can well believe that they exchange words among themselves that my language is poor in, that probably has not even vocabulary for. Why wouldn't it be so? There's no shortage here of intelligence, of feeling, of desire, of want.

It's a funny thing about language. Science has no real idea how it got started, what the first words were, how words got attached to things and actions, and to feelings and ideas. Yet, without language, is anything real? If I find something on the beach and I can't name it, then what is it? If I can't say what it is, is it anything at all? Yes, it's a *thing*, but a nameless thing is the nearest thing to *nothing*. For sure, over time, if it's interesting enough the *thing* will get a name. But until it does, what kind of existence does it have? It only half exists. In a way it's true that nothing can really be said to exist if we have no word for it.

The first words ever spoken most probably were names, like *mama*, *papa*, among the first words a child speaks. But here's the conundrum. Does a child understand the word *mama* because it *has* a mama, or does it have a mama because there's a word for it? Objectively of course the child has a mother and a father regardless of language, but can the child *know* it has a father, for example, if there is no word for it? It's chilling to think *Teeku-mi* has a daughter who might never understand he is her father. Or could she anyway, just because *Teeku-mi is* her father, with or without a word for it? This reminds me of that amusing story about Adam as he was naming the animals. This really tall animal comes along with spindly legs and an immense, elongated neck and Adam ponders what to call it. He turns to Eve and says, *What do you think?* She says, *Well, it looks a lot like a giraffe to me.* He says, *Yeah, to me too. Think that's what I'll call it.* Could it be that's really the way it is? It's true a child understands its mother *as mother* long before the child learns the word *mama*. When the child finally learns the word *mama* it expresses something the child already seems to know, like Adam and the giraffe. And here is *my* conundrum. *Teeku-mi* thinks I am a priest and I am no priest; and he expects me to heal his daughter but I am no miracle worker. Yet if I could somehow get the two of them together and if I could get this little waif to understand who this man is to her, I'd have pulled off a genuine linguistic miracle. Without doubt it would intrigue my colleagues.

In this regard, when I was with *Tolani* earlier, I asked her, *"Tolani-nu,* how *Jakareme* say *'man'?"*

The woman leaned over toward me and pulled the back of her thumb down the length of my palm. "*Kami-so*," she repeated in *Chiroki*.

"And how *Jakareme* say 'mother'?" I asked. (*Kinasi* in *Chiroki*)

Tolani looked away.

"No word for 'mother' in *Jakareme*?" I persisted.

She took my hand and pulled me close, then, gently, with both her hands she caressed my face. "*Kinasi*," she murmured. "*Kinasi*." I understood it to be the gesture of someone who loves you, mother or not.

Then I took her hand. "I have *Jakareme* word for 'father'," I said. I drew my thumb down the length of her palm and then with both hands I caressed her cheeks. "*Kamiso-kinasi*," I said in *Chiroki (man-mother)*.

The woman lying there just stared up at me.

And then I pressed the point, "And Sweet Berry must understand *Teeku-mi* is her father." But the woman closed her eyes at this and turned away. This was more than she wished to deal with. Besides, as far as she knew, the two of them would never meet again.

I sat there by her for a while, reflecting on how fine her features were despite the ravages of her illness, how very like her lovely little Sweet Berry. Before long she drifted off and I did not stay.

My campfire is no more than cinders now and I'm about to turn in. Tomorrow morning I will see *Tolani* first thing and administer another dose of this drug. It appears to be doing the job. Strange, I can't get this *Chiroki* woman off my mind. She is so lovely despite everything. *Teeku-mi* will be stunned to learn that his wife is here. But will he come to her? She abandoned him, and in any case he surely won't come unless he believes the curse has been lifted. How am I to convince him that all we have here is tragic need, *Chiroki* like himself, his own people, even his own family, all needing his eyes and strong hands.

CHAPTER THIRTEEN

HOW THE EXPLORER WINS
THEM OVER

DAY SEVEN: NEW DEVELOPMENTS

IT RAINED DURING THE NIGHT, not a downpour but steady, without let-up. I kept dry enough in my lean-to but this morning it's still coming down, what we'd call back home a country rain. Luckily I have a poncho when I go out on the trail. A campfire is out of the question so breakfast will be meager this morning. Maybe I can grub something from the natives later. I can't leave here without sampling their fare, but what I wouldn't do right now for a cup of strong coffee and a hunk of bread. . . .

A VISIT TO THE CAVE

I am just leaving the cave. When I arrived about twenty minutes ago, the woman was awake. She just kept looking at me, as if to be sure I wasn't something she had dreamt. Or maybe it was the novelty of my poncho, and this hat I am wearing. I smiled at her watching me as I took them off. I could tell someone had already been with her as she had a bowl of untouched food at her side. Her fever is down and already she seems more alert. I asked her how she was feeling but she didn't answer. It's been nine years since she looked upon any-one who could meet her eyes. At one point she smiled back and the light I saw flash in her eyes rather caught me off guard.

I gave her some water and her pill. After she settled back I thought about telling her who I was, where I came from, why I had come up the mountain (*my* reason, not *Teeku-mi's*). I figured I needed to do that to enlist her help with the language project, what time there is left for it. I thought of taking her thin little hand to exercise what I knew so far of the palm language, but I held off. She still seemed too frail and needy. To be honest I enjoyed just being there with her, exchanging shy glanc-es, and every now and then a furtive smile. The silence between us seemed perfectly natural.

The untouched bowl of food beside her caught my eye. I held it up.

"Was Sweet Berry here?" I asked.

"*La*," she replied with a weak but happy smile.

"You want to eat?" I asked, encouraging her.

Slowly she shook her head.

The food was a porridge of some kind, not particularly inviting in appearance, a mash of what looked like pul-verized nuts and crushed, light-colored berries, maybe white current. I tasted it and was surprised at the flavor.

"*Ladi, ladi*" (*very good*), I said, offering her some on a little wooden blade lying there.

She parted her lips and obediently took what was of-fered but after that she turned away.

"Your daughter is also very good," I said trying to keep her engaged. I wanted to say *lovely* but that particular word from Damian's word list escaped me, if it was there at all.

The woman glanced back at me and managed a warm smile. I offered her some water which she took willingly.

"*Jakareme* not have word for daughter, right?" I went on in my hobbled *Chiroki*.

This time there was no smile. "*La*," she answered dryly.

I knew I shouldn't ply her this way but it was now or never.

"And no word for husband also, right?" I asked, leaning closer to her.

She looked at me curiously, almost sharply, but said nothing.

We lapsed back into silence after that, the woman with her face turned away.

Just then I heard sounds at the cave entrance and silhouettes suddenly blocked the daylight. One of them entered, gently tapping his pole before him, the tall, lean figure of the chief. In his other hand he carried a bowl of fruit. Interestingly, he did not bother to tap his code. And he seemed to know just how many steps to take to get by the woman's side. *Tolani* of course heard and saw all this and threw me a look begging me to leave her now. I did just that but at the cave entrance I turned back to see the chief kneeling down beside her, placing his cheek against hers. . . .

I am making my way at this moment down the path from the cave to the chief's compound. It's still coming down, a thin steady rain. Charlie-Two was not at the cave entrance and I hoped I might find him in the chief's enclosure, but I see now that it's empty. I see that the trophy skin he had put out to cure was brought in out of the rain.

I am now on the main trail heading into the women's quarters. No one is out on the trail. Every last soul is hunkered down in their shelters. Some of these poor ladies look wet through, day-long rain seeping down on them through the saturated straw of their roof covering. It's tough. The rainy season is about to begin and life in these flimsy shelters must have its miseries.

Someone is coming down the trail . . .

A REPAIR JOB

I signed off earlier when I saw Charlie-Two and my old friend Damian-Two moving toward me on the trail, both thoroughly soaked. Charlie-Two was in the lead, swinging his cane pole. He had vines wrapped around his waist. Damian-Two behind him had bamboo poles slung over his shoulder and he too had vines coiled around the waist. I let them pass without making contact and began to follow.

The two turned up a path to a women's shelter where I could see part of the roof had caved in. They tapped their arrival to the ladies and obtained their consent to enter, the ladies stepping outside into the rain as they did so. The two set about feeling around for the extent of the damage. The roofing of these shelters is makeshift in the extreme—bamboo stalks laid out over vine lines tied to neighboring trees. The stalks are covered with a thick bed of straw. In this particular shelter, the rain-laden covering snapped some of the vine lines and half the roof spilled down on the occupants.

It was not going to be easy work and I decided to pitch in. The two of course had no idea I was standing just a few feet away. The *Jakareme* are not unused to unexpected brushes from out of nowhere—they can't see what's coming at them after all—but even so it must always be unsettling. I had to finesse my presence, so I reached over and as deftly as possible tapped my identity code on Charlie-Two's pole. He knew at once it was me and instantly thrust his palm out into the empty air. Curiously he did not sway his arm back and forth in the way I would have expected. *Tolani* has obviously talked to the chief about me, so he knows I am like her, and so does his inner circle, that I am able to touch without ever missing the mark. Charlie-Two made Damian-Two aware of my presence and this latter also held out his palm, but he did so in the usual swinging fashion. We of course went through the customary ritual of feeling for each other's identify markers. And Charlie-Two checked my finger for the missing ring. He must know by now the chief has it. It's interesting how crucial these little details are to the *Jakareme*. It's how they take you in, how they lay their eyes on you. My poncho was a mystery to them for sure.

These two had work ahead of them but they've obviously faced this sort of mess before. I jumped in and helped shove the soaked straw off the flooring. We strung new support vines between the trees, lay bamboo stalks across the new lines and then, finally, re-lay the straw covering, wet as it was. I let Charlie-Two lead the effort but I could see and do things these two missed so the repairs went fairly fast and in an hour the roof was restored and the women were back inside, palming their gratitude to the two. They had no notion of my being there.

We spent much of the day inspecting the shelters this way, strengthening and making repairs to roofs. I liked working with these two. The *Jakareme* have their disabilities but one of them is not lack of intelligence. Charlie-Two especially impresses me. I can see why the chief is so fond of him. He must be about the same age as my son, Charlie. He has that same keenness my son had, or *has* I should say. (Why do I speak of him in the past tense?) It was gratifying how easily Charlie-Two and I fell into a neat, relaxed work pattern.

As we made our rounds, I also got to play medic again. At times, soon as we finished our repairs at a given shelter, Damian-Two would bring me a woman with a nasty rash or lesion of some kind. I perform these ministrations always staying at the edge of the shelter. But Damian-Two, curiously enough, would ignore the taboo and go right inside if there was any hesitation on the needy woman's part. I noticed that some of the women were perturbed when he did this but it didn't stop this fellow when help was needed, rather like his namesake I imagine. I see this business is getting to me too. With the little time I have left here, I should be collecting data on their language, and here I am fixing roofs instead. Figure that one out.

It is later in the afternoon and we've covered the

entire camp and pretty much taken care of what was needed. My two partners have left and now I'm on my way back to Sweet Berry's shelter. Thankfully the rain has let up and I've put aside my poncho and lid, hanging them for now on a bamboo tree just off the trail. . . .

I'm at Sweet Berry's now. I see that she is in. And the Dragon Lady also. The two are at the rear of the shelter, palming. The children are playing nearby with what looks like little creeper strings.

I just tapped on the flooring and Sweet Berry tapped back and is coming toward where I am at the shelter's edge. She too is holding her hand straight out without swaying, so *Tolani* has been telling her daughter about me. . . .

A STRANGE EXCHANGE

It is already late in the afternoon as I record what just happened.

Soon as Sweet Berry got to me, we felt for each other's identity strings. Hardly a moment passed before her inquisitive little fingers went back to the relic pouch hanging off my chest—not the first time she's shown interest in it—so I removed the snakeskin pouch and rested it in her hand. She began playing with it, turning it over and over, feeling the hard object inside. Then very suddenly she placed it over her head. Then she really surprised me. She took off her own identity string and feeling out for me, she slipped it over my head. Of all truly remarkable things, she had just exchanged identities with me. These identity strings are everything to the *Jakareme*. It's their name, their face, it says who they are. That she would do something like this very literally stunned me.

But I was pleased she took the relic actually. Her wearing it now, just the way Damian the priest wore it (and this pseudo priest) could be the very thing to bring *Teeku-mi* around. For certain he will be troubled when we meet the day after tomorrow and he sees me without *Odilia sannu*. But seeing *Odilia* on his daughter could make a world of difference.

I was intrigued by the fact that Sweet Berry made no effort to open the pouch since she kept feeling the hard object inside. Perhaps she didn't grasp that it could be opened. But then, suddenly, she stretched out to find my hand and drew it to the relic. Next she tapped twice, rapidly, on the center of my palm. I knew this to be the sign for "tell me". I didn't have the vocabulary to respond, but after a moment I took her little face in my two hands just as her mother had shown me, and touched her palm with the same two rapid strokes. *Your mother will tell.* I felt she understood my gesture for she settled back. Now all I have to do is explain this crazy relic thing to *Tolani* (not that I've been able to do that to myself).

This impulsive exchange that Sweet Berry pulled off was an unexpected gift to me. I've developed an unaccountable urge to help these poor souls, maybe every bit as much as Christopher Damian, strange as that is for me to say. And this crazy relic may be just the thing I need to make that happen. Oddly enough, that's something else I have in common with the priest.

Sweet Berry mustn't think the object in this pouch is a plaything, something to amuse the children with. But I

The nine-year-old Sweet Berry is intrigued with the mysterious object the explorer wears.

don't think I need to worry. Her fingers were already caressing the pouch as something special. Maybe because it was mine, the sign of who I am.

Every bit as important though is how this little girl will react to *Teeku-mi* when I bring him to her. Assuming he'll come. He'll be looking for the miracle but what I am trying to do is miracle enough—persuade him that his delightful little daughter is anything but cursed. That no one here is cursed. And that's where Sweet Berry comes in. It has to start with his daughter. When he touches her, as he'll have to in order to establish his presence, she mustn't pull away. Yet quite naturally she's apt to. She's plenty intuitive. She'll sense his coldness, his hesitations. Somehow, Sweet Berry has to grasp that, no matter, this man is special to her, that he's her father, her man-mother. She has to reach out to him, warm up to him. That just might soften him. A man's daughter can do that. I've pondered this these past nights and am convinced her mother holds the key. If *Tolani* has any feelings left for her husband, Sweet Berry will pick that up. Hasn't it always been that way? The child sees the father through the mother's eyes. That's how I lost my son Charlie.

I intended to take *Odilia sannu* out of its snakeskin pouch and try explaining her to Sweet Berry, but Dragon Lady came up to us just then wanting her for something. This woman could be jealous of the time I spend with her little partner. Anyway, I seized the moment to give Dragon Lady a trinket I've been carrying around for several days, just for her. Taking her hand, I dropped one of my glass necklaces in it. She immediately fingered the beads, trying to grasp what it could be. Then I took the necklace and slipped it over her head, allowing it to fall alongside her identity vine. Both hands flew there at once as she took this in, her manner of looking in a mirror. It took only a moment before it was obvious the gift was pleasing her. She stretched for Sweet Berry and drew the girl's hand to it. Together the fingers of all four hands played over the little beads. Then Sweet Berry did the same, drawing Dragon Lady's hand to her snakeskin pouch. Dragon Lady recognized right away that her little friend was wearing my identity string and that she no longer wore her own. Dragon Lady put two and two together quickly enough and reached out to see that I indeed was wearing her partner's string. This exchange of identities clearly troubled her and she withdrew. She had to think this one over. . . .

Well, I can't do anything about the relic now. It's time for *Tolani's* medication. I am off to the cave.

THE PROMISE

It's early evening and I'm back at my campsite. My head is still spinning from what happened at the cave late this afternoon. When I got there, *Tolani* was wide awake. Her fever had broken and she was looking much better. She was still plenty weak but as soon as she saw me she made an effort to sit up for her pill. She noticed the change on me almost at once and reached over for my new identity string.

"*Lunas-nili?*" she said (*Sweet Berry?*), fingering the knot code.

"*La,*" I said.

"*Kili?*" she asked (*why?*).

"*Lunas-nili* good friend," I said. A warm smile colored the woman's face. I took her hand and said, "*Tolani* friend also, yes?"

Her eyes shaded over as she said, "*La.*" She withdrew her hand and looked away.

"*Tolani*," I said, "Friend want tell something." I had to let this woman know that in two days her husband could be sitting right where I was at that moment.

She glanced back at me a bit warily.

"About *Teeku-mi*, about husband," I said.

"*Teeku-mi*," she repeated uneasily

Leaning in close to her, I said, pointing to myself "*Teeku-mi* bring friend *dundi lano.*"

She looked at me with disbelief.

"*La*, and husband come back soon."

She simply stared at me without a word.

"Is true, *Tolani*," I said. "Husband come *dundi lano* in two days."

"*Teeku-mi?*" she said, a mocking half-smile on her lips.

"*Teeku-mi* come see daughter," I said. "*Teeku-mi* not know *Tolani* here.*"

Then abruptly, her chest heaving, she burst out, "No! *Teeku-mi* not come." She almost laughed. "Only *Jakareme* here," she said.

"Yes," I said, "Maybe true, maybe not come." Pointing to myself, I added, "But friend try bring."

She studied me for a time, eyes pulled in skeptically, then she asked, "*Kili?*"

I had only half the words I needed to explain why. "*Tolani*," I started, "*Tolani* know about *Odilia sannu?*"

She looked at me perplexed. *"Odilia sannu?"* she said.

"La, Odilia sannu," I said. *"Tolani* remember about *Katalan,* long time ago? *Katalan* come on river, bring *Odilia sannu."* Then I added, "Maybe *Tolani* not born yet."

After a moment she said quietly, *"La."*

"And *Tolani* know when husband born, *Teeku-mi,* son of *Matsitu,* he also *Jakareme?"*

Again an almost inaudible, *"La."*

"And *Tolani* know *Odilia sannu* cure *Teeku-mi,* yes?" I stated rather than asked, for I was certain she knew.

Her eyes softened as she absorbed this but she did not speak. She did not have to. All the *Chiroki* knew of *Odilia sannu.* They all knew the legend of the cure. That painful pseudo-Mass before a thousand *Chiroki,* just a week ago, left no doubt how these aborigines felt about *Odilia.* Watching her, I was certain she was no different. And it was precisely this native superstition I hoped to exploit.

What happened next, I am embarrassed to say, had me playing the priest once again. *"Tolani,"* I began, *"Odilia sannu* is very powerful, yes?"

"La," she said softly.

"More strong than *Jaka (curse),* yes?"

She only half-nodded, her eyes asking, *What are you telling me?*

I went on, "Long time ago, *Katalan* leave *Chiroki.* Take *Odilia sannu* away, on river, yes?"

Again she half-nodded. She knew the story.

I leaned closer and again pointing to myself, I said, "Now friend come on river, bring *Odilia sannu* back."

I cannot find words to describe her reaction to this, like something had hit her. She just lay there peering at me. Finally, pointing at me, she said, "You *Katalan?*"

"*La*," I said.

"*Katalan* have *Odilia sannu?*" she asked, trying to absorb this.

"*Katalan* now no have *Odilia sannu*," I said, and then delivered what I knew would be the real shocker. "*Odilia sannu* now with daughter. *Lunas-nili* have *Odilia sannu.*"

It was as if she hadn't heard me, or couldn't comprehend, so I went on.

"Around neck," I said, gesturing to the identity string around my own neck. "*Odilia sannu* stay with daughter now." As I spoke these words, I realized how impossible all this had to sound to this poor woman. I reached to take her hand but she kept it from me.

"*Lunas-nili?*" she whispered, peering at Sweet Berry's identity string on me.

"*La*," I said, affecting a smile. "Daughter now have *Odilia sannu.*"

"*Kili?*" she whispered.

"*Odilia sannu* want remove *jaka*," I said. It sounded dishonest putting it to her this way, knowing how she would interpret it, but I had little choice.

Her eyes narrowed as she peered at me. *Tolani* put her hands to her eyes and said, "Cure blind?"

I hesitated, at a loss what to say. Sweet Berry's blindness is not going away. What I want this dear woman to understand, and *Teeku-mi* and all the *Chiroki*, is that blindness and deafness are not curses. This mountain is not cursed. There are no evil spirits on *dundi lano*. If they

161

could understand this that would be my miracle. And I believe it will happen. The logic is there. If *Odilia* now belongs to the *Jakareme*, then these poor souls can't be *Jakareme* any more. And if they aren't *Jakareme*, there is no reason for them to be kept apart like this, not one day longer.

I could not lie to this woman, but I could answer what I truly believed, "*Odilia sannu* remove curse."

Tolani's frail body seemed to collapse at these words. Her eyes began to brim with tears. For a long time no word was spoken. She would glance up at me and turn away, and then look back, eyes probing, *Is this really so?*

Finally she said, "Is true?"

"*La,*" I said simply. "Is true."

I wondered what I had done, raising hopes for her kind of miracle that was not going to be. And, truthfully, things could go wrong, my plan could blow up in my face. But somehow I truly believed *Teeku-mi* would come and that the uncanny logic attached to this amazing relic would hold.

We stayed that way for a long time, neither of us speaking but each very much alive to the other's presence. To this poor woman, I was a reincarnation of that miracle-working priest legend she had heard about as she grew up. And to me she was this frail, sickly woman with more metal in her than a *Chiroki* warrior. And so appealingly tender and warm. I envied *Teeku-mi* for his good fortune in such a wife. And for his daughter too, so obviously cut from the same lovely cloth. I will never understand how he let them go. He had to have known

Tolani followed her daughter to *dundi lano*. Why didn't he go after her? Their fear is so irrational. And there's the irony of it all. Here's this fantasy of terror that has the *Chiroki* paralyzed, and here's this bone chip of a dead woman from halfway around the world about to liberate them. And all this because of an imposter priest who happens to scorn both the curse they fear and the miracle they dream of. Why am I even recording this? I'll never be able to relate any of this to my peers. And here's the strangest part: this sense I have that what I am doing is something I have been brought here to do and have no choice but to carry out. Who will believe it? Can I believe it myself?

Our silent spell together was sweet but it did not last. Before long the chief and his underlings appeared at the cave entrance. This time Charlie-Two came in with the chief. Both were carrying bowls of food, apparently supper for *Tolani* and themselves. As soon as *Tolani* saw the chief she made an effort to raise herself. He sat down beside her and feeling for her, placed his cheek against hers and drew her to himself. After a moment she gently edged him away, glancing at me with a funny smile. But this time her glance did not ask me to leave. She began palming the chief, a long exchange, which ended when he stretched out his hand looking for me. I took it, happily noting that he still wore the ring, and in customary fashion touched his identity string. He reached out for mine and then, confused at what he found, felt for my beard. He turned and began palming *Tolani*. Again, another long exchange between the two of them. Meanwhile, Charlie-Two merely sat there oblivious to any of this. After a while he began to pick at his food. I wanted him to know I was there so I took a rock and tapped my code on the cave floor near him and instantly he reached out to find me. He too quickly discovered the change in my identity string, and was no less puzzled. I palmed the sign for *is OK* and then withdrew my hand. I would not know how to answer any of his signs back to me and had to leave him to his thoughts.

When *Tolani* and the chief were done with their conversation, he held out his bowl to me. *Tolani* smiled and nodded for me to accept it. It was no little gesture for the chief to do something like this. I took the bowl and palmed my thanks. The chief then began palming his young aide as *Tolani* and I waited, exchanging glances. When the chief was finished, *Tolani* handed him her bowl and right away he began his meal. She nodded to me that I should also. I was hungry but the food did not look the least appetizing—a concoction of legumes and mashed root or tuber of some kind, mixed with chopped plant stalks. The whole thing tasted rather bitter and I had to force myself. But this was their daily fare, what they lived on and kept them alive. I offered my bowl to *Tolani* but she had no interest, only for water which she took readily.

While the others were eating in their silent world, I said to *Tolani*, pointing to myself, "Friend leave here after tomorrow."

She did not seem to understand.

"*Teeku-mi* come soon take friend *Chiroki* village. Friend go on river."

"*Kili?*" she asked, her eyes narrowing.

"But *Odilia sannu* stay here," I said affecting a smile. "With daughter."

She just peered at me, trying to understand.

"Is OK," I went on. "Maybe *Teeku-mi* stay here also."

When she glanced over at the chief, I knew there was some truth in what I had guessed about them. It was probably more on the chief's part than hers, but who knows. In any event, the return of a husband presented a problem I hadn't foreseen. For the *Chiroki* to come here and help these poor souls, there would have to be abundant good will on all sides. And it would have to start with *Teeku-mi.* He has to feel good about what he finds here. And the *Jakareme,* for their part have to open up and trust what is likely to start happening to them. And that openness has to start with this chief, this local *Sabuknu.*

"*Teeku-mi* help *Jakareme,*" I said to her, perhaps with less conviction that I would have liked.

Tolani kept looking at me but said nothing.

Charlie-Two and the chief started palming again. Then the youth palmed *Tolani* and got on his feet. He reached over toward me. I put my hand by his and he palmed the goodbye sign. I had the feeling it would be a good idea if I joined him, but I held us both back. I wanted to ask the chief for a favor, something that had been on my mind all during the meal, something that would involve both the chief and his young protégé.

Turning to *Tolani,* I said, "Tell *Sabuknu* friend very glad *Sabuknu* share meal today."

She did this and the chief palmed something back. The woman smiled at me and said, "*Sabuknu* say you true friend now."

"Tell *Sabuknu,*" I said, "true friend want make special

meal for *Sabuknu* tomorrow." She looked at me quizzically. "*Tolani* tell," I repeated.

Tolani did so and the chief palmed back his assent which she passed on to me with an uneasy, puzzled look.

I pointed to Charlie-Two. "Meal for assistant also. *Tolani* tell," I said. I led the youth over to her and she proceeded to inform him.

"And *Tolani*," I said. "*Tolani* come too. Tomorrow *Tolani* feel better."

The woman barely smiled at this, but I was more than satisfied. Matters were turning out well. I stood up, along with Charlie-Two, and palmed the chief with the customary sign, making a special point of touching the ring on his finger. I looked over at *Tolani* but she would not meet my eyes now. As we left the cave I did not care to look back at the two of them alone.

CHAPTER FOURTEEN

AN INCREDIBLE DAY

DAY EIGHT

TODAY IS MY LAST FULL DAY HERE. Early tomorrow at first light I am certain *Teeku-mi* will show up at the drop-off site looking for me, expecting to see in my face a sign that his daughter has been healed, that *Katalan* and *Odilia sannu* have worked their great miracle, that little Sweet Berry will behold her father now and hear his voice for the first time. And that of course is my dilemma. The moment this aborigine finds that I have come to him alone he will know something is not right. Why haven't I brought his daughter to him? That's where I expect *Odilia* will come in yet again to save the day. *Teeku-mi* will spot quickly enough that *Katalan* is not wearing *Odilia sannu* over his heart. And I will tell him that there is good news and he must come to see, that *Odilia sannu* is staying with his daughter, and that *Odilia sannu* has lifted the curse. I will tell him every last evil spirit has fled from *dundi lano,* that the *jaka* is no more and the *Jakareme* now must have a new name. But miracles no doubt wear a special face and he will not see that special face in mine. And he will be troubled. And I can't pretend any more than I have already. Still, he will trust what *Katalan* tells him, and he will come, I am fairly certain of that, particularly when he hears that his daughter carries *Odilia sannu* in the way of *Katalan*. He will not understand any of this but he will come. And then, who knows, things will go well or they won't.

I still have much to do. I still have to prepare little Sweet Berry for this meeting with her father, with her *man-mother*. And I have to prepare the chief for the presence of a new alien in this little world of his, and for the inevitable turmoil that is bound to happen when *Teeku-mi* gets here. And then for the hardest part, that this newcomer is *Tolani's* man. And there's *Tolani* herself. How she will receive *Teeku-mi,* and for that matter how will he look upon the woman who abandoned him nine years ago?

Why do I care? Why I am doing these things? I am hard put to say, and I confess it puzzles me not a little. I am a linguist and I came up to the *Jakareme* to satisfy a linguist's curiosity, nothing more, and now here I find myself putting aside my research, fretting instead about these poor people's welfare. It's as if some mysterious, hidden purpose has ruled this entire adventure from the start, in accord with some inexplicable inner logic of its own. The logic, whatever it is, mystifies me no end, but I can well imagine the good Reverend linguist Christopher Damian is enjoying a good chuckle over it. I have to laugh myself at what's happened. Perhaps I'm simply another of these little miracles *Odilia sannu* keeps springing on me.

Anyway, I will be going to *Tolani* shortly. She holds the key to what has to happen now, or at least after

Odilia herself. I must get her to talk to Sweet Berry about her father. And to the chief about her husband. Two tall orders for someone who may not be the least bit pleased to see the world she left behind moving back in on her. . . .

Sitting here over my breakfast (coffee, powdered eggs, no fried biscuits this morning, to conserve flour), I've been thinking about the dinner party I plan to throw for the chief later today. It was the right thing to do, to tie up the loose ends. For sure I have to prepare him and the others for change. A meal with enticing new flavors is not a bad way to set this up. Give these poor souls a foretaste of good things to come.

EVENTS OF THE EIGHTH DAY
RECORDED TWO DAYS LATER

I am on my way down Lost Mountain in the company of two *Chiroki* warriors, without their war paint now. I did not have an opportunity to record events as they occurred these past two days, so much went on, so I will do so now for as long as I am able. (I am down to my last set of batteries.)

We have just stopped for an overnight camp near the base of the mountain, not more than a day's journey to the *Chiroki* village where this all began just ten days ago. The two *Chiroki* warriors who have been leading me are both asleep by our campfire. These strong, stalwart aborigines were only on the edge of events that took place yesterday morning, but still they knew something important had happened. *Teeku-mi* had given these two strict orders to lead *Katalan* back down to *Sabuknu*. He instructed them to treat me with the highest respect. *Teeku-mi* even bowed low to me in front of them. I'm embarrassed to say this but if I was venerated by the *Chiroki* before, I have become like a god to them now. And indeed, just before the two of them turned in, they came before me and touched their heads to the earth.

For reasons that I will relate, *Teeku-mi* and his other guards are staying behind.

The events I report here are so unheard of, so hard to believe that they must seem unreal, but I record them now exactly as they occurred, beginning two days ago.

MORNING OF THE EIGHTH DAY

Early on the morning of the eighth day of my adventure among the *Jakareme*, I went to the cave to administer *Tolani's* medicine and to try and get her to speak to her daughter Sweet Berry and to the chief, to prepare each of them for *Teeku-mi's* imminent arrival. When I got to the cave two of the chief's underlings were at the entrance, so it was clear he was inside. I slipped by them and found the chief sitting by her, or more accurately *near* her, not so close now. He was eating. I watched him for a while for he seemed different, withdrawn and distant, as if he and the woman near him were in separate worlds. *Tolani* for her part was dozing. There was a bowl of food by her that had been touched but only barely. I took her hand and held it until she woke up. She took the medicine but she avoided my gaze and she too seemed preoccupied. I watched her glance over at the chief, seemingly satisfied that he was unaware of my presence.

"*Tolani*," I said quietly, though I hardly needed to keep my voice down. She looked up at me.

"*Tolani* remember?" I said. "Tomorrow, *Teeku*-mi come take friend back *Chiroki* village."

"*La,*" she nodded, rather coolly I thought.

Then I asked, "*Tolani* want friend bring *Teeku-mi*?" I did not know the *Chiroki* word for *cave* so I pointed to the ground. She understood me well enough.

After a long silence she whispered so weakly I could barely make it out, "*La.*"

I took her hand again. "*Tolani*," I said, "chief must know, yes?"

She withdrew her hand with a delicacy that rather affected me. "Chief know," she said.

I looked over at the chief. He had finished his meal and seemed adrift in thought.

"Chief know husband come?" I asked.

"Chief know," she said, looking over at him almost with pain in her eyes. I wondered how she managed *husband*, but what went on between them was their business.

We sat there for a while saying nothing. Then the chief seemed to come to himself. He leaned over and touched *Tolani*, tentatively, not looking for a response, and then he grasped his seeing-eye cane in one hand and his bowl in the other and got on his feet. The two of us watched as the old figure, in slow deliberate steps, picked his way out of the cave.

Tolani looked at me, her eyes wet. She seemed so

frail and needy, I wanted to take her hand, but I held back. She too was preparing for the emotional storm about to break over her.

But there was one more thing I needed from her. "*Tolani*," I said, "Sweet Berry also must know, yes?"

Tolani managed a weak smile. "*Tolani* tell," she said quietly.

"Sweet Berry understand *father*?" I asked.

She looked straight at me. "Father like *man-mother*," she said, managing a sly grin.

I had to laugh at that myself.

She was tired now. Before long she drifted off and I left the cave.

I took the path down to Sweet Berry's dwelling. I was still worried about her. This little girl had no idea what it was she had taken from me so impulsively like that. God knows the object she slung so hastily around her neck was not an ornament, or some sort of identity string, not even of me. For all I knew this thing could become a stick of dynamite. How would this aborigine react when he realizes that *Odilia sannu* hasn't worked her magic, that his daughter still sees nothing, still can't hear a word he says. There was no telling what he'd do. He might think the magic object had lost its power, or that *Odilia sannu* did not listen to this *Katalan*, or that I had simply deceived him and worse, made a fool of this *Chiroki* crown prince.

But I kept a positive mind about this. *Odilia* after all cured *Teeku-mi* once upon a time, if I can believe that. Anyway, my hope was that his simple faith in *Odilia* would survive, that once he saw that *Odilia* now belonged to the *Jakareme*, to his own daughter in fact, he would believe that the evil spirits had fled. The dread these *Chiroki* had of the Lost Mountain would melt away and when it did, the cruel isolation of these accursed people would end. That would be miracle enough. To be sure, I knew it might end differently. But somehow I never seriously doubted this was going to turn out well. All because of this crazy relic of some unknown saint. When I thought of all the weird twists and turns that have taken place up to this point because of her, the uncanny way she has of making the most improbable things happen, I had no reason to doubt she would finish what-ever it was she started. My place was simply to let this *Odilia* have her way. I have to admit I hardly recognized myself in these thoughts. How could a man of science and an avowed agnostic think this way? Good question. There I was, scientific work abandoned, scheming to help these poor, benighted souls, and banking on the bone of a long-dead woman to pull it off. What can I say? It's beyond explaining.

When I got to Sweet Berry's enclosure, she and the Dragon Lady were out somewhere on the trail with the children. I would have to make time for her later. As it was I had enough to do to get ready for my farewell party. I was resolved this at least would come off well. But, as it turned out, even that had its quotient of un-foreseeable twists and turns.

It was mid-morning when I got back to my camp. I spent an hour in the surrounding thicket hunting for game for the party. I felt confident I could shoot a small boar or if not that then I'd bag some edible birds. I'd seen plover, snipe and even parrots in the underbrush there. But nothing came of this forage. So I had to content myself with pond carp. And I didn't do so well even there. The pond that morning was lifeless, netting me a paltry catch. But the party's small and I felt it would be enough. And for once their carp would be fried and nicely seasoned.

In all the time that I had been among the *Jakareme*, I never saw any evidence of fire. I doubt they know what fire is. Perhaps there have been jungle fires in their long history, but I saw no evidence of anything having to do with fire. Everything they eat is either raw or cooked by the sun. Something roasted, fried or oven-baked is beyond them. At the party, at least the chief and his buddies will get a foretaste of better fare to come.

I had ingredients enough for two small loaves of bread. (It's strange to think no *Jakareme* had ever tasted the staple of life.) There are a number of ways to make bread over an open fire. One can fry dough in a little oil, as I had been doing most mornings. But for the party my one frying pan was for the fish, so I turned to my coffee pot. I'd done this before. You pile hot coals all around the can so that it functions like a Dutch oven. Crude but it works.

THE PARTY

After I mixed the flour, water, and baking soda, etc., and kneaded two small loaves, and then cleaned the carp, I gathered hardwood and carted the lot to the chief's compound. There I built a fireplace in the clearing just a few yards from the chief's enclosure, using stones hauled up from the brook. Then I started the fire. The chief and his underlings were in, but as yet they had no inkling any of this was taking place just a few steps away, though the smell of burning wood must have mystified them some.

It was early afternoon by then and party time was approaching. I went up to the cave to get *Tolani*. I would need her translating skills, and frankly, I wanted her with me, someone I could make eye contact with. When I got to the cave I found Sweet Berry by her mother and the two were palming in deep conversation. *Tolani* was sitting up (her condition was improving every day). She saw me come in but did not immediately turn from her daughter. I was glad to see them together. But as I sat there waiting in the dim cave light, I noticed that Sweet Berry had opened the pouch and was holding the relic in her hand. I was going to have her replace it when suddenly, what happened next rather astonished me. Sweet Berry reached up for her mother's face and gently put the relic to her lips to kiss it. And then she brought it to her own lips and kissed it herself, doing so in the most tender way imaginable. At this *Tolani* drew her daughter into her arms and kissed her. *Tolani* glanced over at me with a look as lovely as any I have ever seen in a woman. Not on my account, I hasten to add.

Tolani let Sweet Berry know I was there and the instant she realized this, the little girl stretched out her hand. When I started to palm her she pulled me close and feeling for my mouth, placed *Odilia* squarely on my lips. I too was to kiss *Odilia*. And in fact, with *Tolani* looking on, that's exactly what I did; *Katalan* could hardly do otherwise. And here I thought I was to teach this little tyke about the relic. *Tolani* must have been telling her that the thing she bore on her heart was magical. But would regard for magic give rise to kisses? Would this little girl even understand the notion of magic? And there's something else. Why did she insist on having this thing in the first place, the very moment she felt *Odilia* on me? At the time I figured she wanted it as a memento, but if that's so, then why would she have *me* kiss it? This was only the first of the inexplicables that took place between *Odilia* and this little girl, as I shall shortly relate.

At that point, though, I had no time to dwell on any of this. Party time was nearing and there was bread to bake and fish to fry. *Tolani* was much too weak to walk, so I had the pleasure of carrying her down to the party site I had prepared by the chief's compound. Sweet Berry felt her way along the vine line behind us. I took Charlie-Two's animal skin curing there in the sun and made a bed for *Tolani,* right by the fireplace. The chief and his four underlings were in the enclosure, still oblivious to any of this, engaged it seemed in business as usual with some community members.

I had good supply of red hot coals by now and it was time for the chief to be brought in. From *Tolani* I learned the *Jakareme* sign for *come* and then tapped my code on the chief's floor and made contact with him. He seemed surprised but when I palmed the *come* sign he let me lead him off the edge of his enclosure. I brought him to *Tolani.* The chief was not a little shocked I think to find her there, but he put it all together quickly enough. I laid out right by her the animal skin from the cave, the one that I had given him, hoping he would take it well. I had *Tolani* ask the chief to have Charlie-Two alert the

Sweet Berry offers the relic for the explorer to kiss.

Dragon Lady of the impending party, and also Damian-Two. The chief's compound was the only one the two genders can ever meet in and become aware of each other, so there was no problem with mixed company for this party. Charlie-Two was coming of course. I didn't see how I could exclude the other underlings, so the food would have to stretch.

Tolani sat there watching as I added wood for frying the fish. She hadn't seen a fire in nine years and she was visibly fascinated as the flames shot up. But her reaction was nothing like the chief and his underlings who were utterly mystified by the fire's heat and the smells of burning. *Tolani* took it upon herself to palm the chief what was happening. I have no idea how she managed the notion of *fire,* but she's as smart as she is lovely. No wonder one gets taken with her. After that little exchange, though, I never saw the two of them palming again. Soon as he got back, she drew Charlie-Two in between them and from that point on, whenever I gave *Tolani* something to tell the chief, she would pass it through this underling.

As we sat there watching the fire, I asked her about certain terms I would need. For one, I needed to know how to refer to myself. How did the *Jakareme* sign me? She held back a laugh and said they signed me *hair face.*

"How *Jakareme* say *Tolani*?" I asked. Here she hesitated then looked at me and shook her head.

"Only chief and daughter know *Tolani*?" I asked.

"*La,*" she said half-smiling.

"*Tolani* have *Jakareme* name?" I asked. She did not want to answer though I'm sure the chief has given her one.

"Sweet Berry have name?" I asked.

Tolani's face brightened. "Sweet Berry name *Happy*," she said taking my hands and swooping them together in the way anyone does anywhere when pleased.

"Sweet Berry happy because Sweet Berry have good mother," I said. *Tolani* said nothing to this but of course this is true. Little Sweet Berry is the only one here who knows her mother, who even knows what a mother is, the only one as far as I knew who ever remembers a mother's touch.

"*Tolani*," I said, "how speak about *Odilia sannu?*"

She looked at me puzzled. "*Kili?*" she asked quietly. Why did I want to?

I was not sure how to answer. "*Tolani*," I said at length, "*Odilia sannu* bring friend here, bring *hair face*." Peering right into her eyes with as much conviction as I could summon up, I said, "*Odilia sannu* want take away *Jakareme* curse."

She stared at me with a vacant look. I had said these things to her before in the cave, but now an almost angry skepticism crept into those eyes. "*Ko asum?*" she asked dryly (*And how?*). I have to admit the unfamiliar hardness in her tone hurt. She was an ally but there were limits.

"We see," I said. I knew she wasn't buying it. Why should she? This *Odilia sannu* had done nothing so far to relieve their unhappy lot.

"We see?" *Tolani* repeated with a weary, scornful edge to her voice.

"*La*," I said, forcing myself. "We see."

THE MYSTERIOUS FEEDING

I should have realized the aroma of baking bread and frying fish would make mincemeat of my guest list. These people have hypersensitive olfactory nerves and the unfamiliar smells of baking bread were bound to draw everyone in the camp. And that's exactly what happened. Little by little, their seeing-eye poles sweeping low before them, virtually the entire community drifted into the courtyard and arranged themselves along the vine lines, men on one side, women on the other. It was a sad state of affairs for there wasn't going to be any food for this crowd. I had barely enough for the chief and these chosen few.

I spotted Damian-Two and the Dragon Lady as they poled their way in, and I went over and led them to a place around the fire. They at least ought to have a taste. *Tolani* palmed each of them so they would know what was happening. She also palmed Charlie-Two with messages for the chief, keeping him abreast of each development. She was very proper that way, about the chief's right to know. But as I said, I never saw anything more between them after that. He seemed OK about it and even seemed up for the party. I couldn't say the same for *Tolani*. Mostly she kept to Sweet Berry, letting her know what the smells meant, what I was doing, that the whole community was gathering in the courtyard. Sweet Berry for her part looked happy as could be. She seemed to have a lively sense of everyone's presence. I could not help but notice that she was clutching *Odilia* in her little hands. Little did I fathom what was passing through her mind.

My timing was near perfect. The second loaf of bread finished baking just as I got through frying the fish. And so, finally now, the meal was ready to distribute. I had brought down some bowls earlier from the pile in the cave and I proceeded to fill one with a good piece of fish and a man-sized hunk of bread for the chief. Then I prepared bowls for *Tolani,* Sweet Berry and the Dragon Lady, and heaped up bowls for Charlie-Two and Damian-Two, and finally a bit for myself. And that was it; there was nothing for anyone else, as it turned out not even for the underlings.

But what actually happened confounds belief. Frankly, I'll never understand it. The meal started out normally enough. The chief had an appetite and seemed to enjoy putting away his meal, but then of a sudden he passed his bowl on to one of his underlings, and he too dug in at once with obvious pleasure. But then, like his chief, he passed the bowl to another of the underlings. The others around the fire also looked like they were relishing every bite, especially Charlie-Two, but after a while he got up with the bowl and with one arm swaying out before him made his way over to one of the lines and gave it to the first person he came up against. *Tolani* didn't even touch hers and when he came back she passed hers to him, and this he took to another of the lines. Sweet Berry and the Dragon Lady ate well I thought but then they did the same, passing it to one or another of the underlings who felt his way to the lines with it. And that's how it went down each of the lines. When anyone received the bowl, he or she would eat and then pass it back to the one behind. And when the end of the line was finished and the bowls were passed back up to the front, none was completely empty, Yet everyone had eaten. I was watching. Everyone, about seventy of them, enjoyed himself or herself and there was still leftover food. Most perplexing thing I've ever witnessed.

THE ADDRESS

When this extraordinary, utterly inexplicable feeding was over, I motioned to *Tolani* to inform the chief I had something to tell him, and that I would like him to pass my words on to the others.

The chief nodded and I got on my feet to face him, most unnecessarily I might add, and using simple, almost kindergarten sentences to make things easy for *Tolani*, I began:

Hair face friend want tell important news.

I waited for *Tolani* to palm these words to Charlie-Two. How she handled these words I'll never know but she did. Charlie-Two quickly passed the words on to the chief who then did the same to one of the other underlings and from there it spread like ripples in a pond. There was no way of telling what was happening to these words as they got passed along.

I went on: *Have very good news. New friend come tomorrow. New friend want meet chief.*

I watched for the chief to get this, then added,

New friend bring many good things. New friend help everyone. New friend make everyone happy.

And that was the last word I got to utter. From that point on I have to say *Odilia sannu* took charge.

First it was Sweet Berry. As soon as *Tolani* palmed her the word *happy*, this little girl sprang up as though an electric current had passed through her body. With *Odilia* clutched in her hand she felt her way past her mother to Charlie-Two and began palming him. And then, just as she had done to me earlier in the cave, she brought *Odilia* to his lips. After that she moved on to the chief and did the same, palming him at some length, and he too was given *Odilia* to kiss. Whether the chief did or not I could not tell, but he handed Sweet Berry over to the underlings, and after kissing *Odilia*, the last of the underlings took her to the lines. She worked her way down the first line, palming each person for a few moments and then offering *Odilia* to be kissed. The spectacle of this little girl moving from person to person in this way had me totally, utterly mesmerized. *Tolani* next to me watched with tears in her eyes.

Then suddenly her little daughter stopped and lifted her head the way people do when they hear a strange, distant sound. Others around her did too. It was not sounds of course but an odor. Those near where I was were unaware at first of any new smells, nor was I. But all the *Jakareme* farther back in the lines began sniffing at the air. And very soon animated palming spread. It wasn't long before the chief became aware of the growing excitement and . . .

CHAPTER FIFTEEN

THE RETURN

Daisy here again. The explorer's account broke off at this point, very likely because his batteries died, as he had forewarned us. My father had to pick up the tale from this point on. How he knew these details is beyond me, but I believe he had access to notes the explorer wrote by hand as he rode the river current back down to the coast.

THE WOMAN *TOLANI* KNEW INSTANTLY what this smell meant. She touched the explorer with great delicacy and said, "New *Jakareme* baby come." Before long he too detected the faint odor of burnt Eucalyptus. *Teeku-mi* evidently had a huge bonfire going at the drop-off. He would have warriors with him too, and given the fire, very likely a *Jakareme* child. But this was only day eight. Why a day early like this? Didn't he understand their arrangement? Was it a failure of trust? Did the stark reality of this new *Jakareme* baby shake his simple faith that *Katalan* would heal his daughter of silence and darkness? That may be so. *Teeku-mi* always had certain doubts about this second *Katalan*. He had them right from the start. Perhaps he sensed that something was not right about the intruder he encountered on the river, this alien who presented himself as a priest.

Whatever, to *Teeku-mi* the miracle was everything,

the only thing. And as far as the explorer knew, there wasn't going to be any miracle. Not a real miracle that let Sweet Berry see what she had never seen, listen to sounds she had never heard. No miracle, and yet, at that moment, how this agnostic soul, this settled man of science wished it might be so. Without the miracle, the *Chiroki* dread of the *jaka* might very well remain as strong as ever. Without the miracle, the explorer's perfect plan could fall apart in an instant. Still, there was reason to hope, wasn't there? He would get *Teeku-mi* to come. He was certain of that. And when *Teeku-mi* spotted *Odilia sannu* being borne over the heart of his little girl, and he saw how very sweet she was, miracle or no miracle. . . and then when he lays his eyes upon his wife, who knows what he will do? Frail as *Tolani* was, he could not deny her loveliness nor fail to see that the *jaka* had done her no harm in nine years, this comely wife of his who braved *dundi lano* with more courage than he. Who knows, it might just be enough.

In the excitement roused by the faint, pungent smell wafting over the camp, the explorer saw the Dragon Lady, pole stretched out before her, feeling her way toward the chief's enclosure. *Tolani* observed her too and explained that she is the one who must go for the baby. New babies were her responsibility. The Dragon Lady was by the chief now and appeared to be getting instructions. It also looked like a detail was being organized to accompany her, led by Charlie-Two. The explorer saw only disaster in this arrangement and he had to stop it. When he spotted his chance, he brought Charlie-Two over to *Tolani* and had her tell him that only *hair face* friend must go for the baby. That *hair face* friend must go alone. Charlie-Two was told to tell this to the chief, which he did in the company of the explorer. After some hesitation, the chief agreed. It seemed this was just one more thing out of his control now.

The Dragon Lady was not happy with this but the chief stood his ground. The explorer thanked him but the chief was unresponsive. By then the order had already gone out for everyone to return to their dwellings, and when the explorer got back to *Tolani*, the courtyard was empty. Her manner too seemed unresponsive. The woman struck him as preoccupied, deep in thought.

With her quiet consent, the explorer lifted *Tolani* into his arms and carried her up to the cave, Sweet Berry again picking her way along behind them. Once mother and daughter were inside and settled down, the explorer made to leave but something in *Tolani's* look asked him to stay. He could see something was troubling her but he had no stomach for whatever it was. He had had more than enough for one day. Seeing he was about to depart, she held out *Odilia* for him to take. That stopped him. Sweet Berry was to have the relic, not her. He pointed to the pouch around the little girl's neck and gestured the woman was to return it there. *Tolani* paid no heed to his instruction, but clearly there was something she wanted. Something in her look was enough to hold him, a long, examining gaze. And then, abruptly, she held the relic not out to him but to her own lips and kissed it. Not looking at him any further, she began stroking the relic's glass face tenderly with one finger. She kept this up for a minute or more, peering down hard at *Odilia*. And then, finally, looking up and turning to her daughter, she placed her finger on Sweet Berry's eyes, first the one and then the other. She repeated this ritual again and again, glancing up at the explorer now each time she moved from eye to eye. As she gazed up at him, her look at first flashed bright with hope and expectation, but then, slowly, that look grew darker and before long turned accusing. He had stirred up that hope in her, never reflecting that a moment of truth like this was bound to come. As she kept on with this ritual, her look grew harder. Not a little unsettling for him. The woman had come to mean too much and bitterness was the last thing he wanted from her. And then as he watched, he saw an expression of outright contempt creep across her face. Then, of a sudden, her hand went limp and the relic fell to the floor of the cave.

The explorer leapt to pick it up and as he did, it appears something happened to him. He alluded to it only once in the notes he left, likening what he felt just then to the bolt you get when you take an extra deep swig of potato vodka or something—a burning flush through your body and then in the next instant you're practically taken out of yourself. Not that he lost consciousness. Just the opposite. But what he did next was hardly him. He picked up the relic and kneeling beside Sweet Berry placed it ever so tenderly on her eyes, first one and then the other as he had seen *Tolani* do. He held *Odilia* on each eye for a long time. He wanted to pray but he couldn't. But at that very moment the priest Damian came to mind and somehow, in his heart, this priest prayed the prayer he himself was incapable of. That this little girl would be healed. *Tolani* watched all this. She watched the explorer's eyes close. She knew what prayer was and knew that this *Katalan* was praying for her daughter. She began to unbend. She placed her slender hand on his, on the hand he held over Sweet Berry's eyes, first one and then the other. And indeed there was prayer, long and ardent prayer, prayer with the faith of a real priest, a priest who offered his life, his death in fact, for the well-being of these tragic souls, the Reverend Father Christopher Damian, S.J. Indeed, for a telling while the explorer seemed to become this priest, offering himself for this little girl and her loving mother. That God would perform a miracle. On his own, the explorer could never say he believed in any of this. But in that moment, outside himself, he believed in the priest Damian, and this priest believed in a miracle-working saint, and this saint believed in a God of miracles, a God who could do anything He wished. It's what makes a saint a saint and even an agnostic man of science had to acknowledge this. At a certain point in life, like at this moment, even one such as he would trust that it must be so.

But none of this passed through his head in those moments. He was not himself. For those fleeting moments he had been the Jesuit Damian. When he came to, back to himself, he realized what he had been doing and in utter confusion abruptly leapt up and fled the cave. Outside he stopped. *Odilia* was still in his hands. He had to go back and give it to her. Sweet Berry's having it on her was the nub of his stratagem. When he re-entered the cave, the girl was in her mother's arms, the two swaying back and forth. *Tolani*'s face was wet with tears, glistening happy tears. When she saw him come back, *Tolani* immediately stretched out her hand, but the explorer never noticed. He thrust the relic into the snakeskin pouch around Sweet Berry and ran out. He never stopped until he got to his camp and threw himself on the ground of his lean-to, thoroughly rattled and exhausted.

He did not sleep that night. At first light he would go to the drop-off point, but that was hours and hours away and the night was long. As he lay there, past events flashed through his mind. He saw himself in the library stacks at his university, chancing upon Damian's manuscript. He heard *Teeku* pronouncing the *Chiroki* words of Damian's list from Carlito's father. Suddenly he was on the river rehearsing simple sentences in this strange new language. Then the delicate little face of Sweet Berry, the way she was when he laid eyes on her the first time, and her sweet little hand signing *Jakareme* words on his palm. And *Tolani*. Always *Tolani*. Her tender face was never really absent from his mind. And the others too, the chief, Charlie-Two, all of them. At one point he got up and started listening to *Teeku's* voice pronouncing the words in Damian's list. And like Damian he began to list all the *Jakareme* signs he had learned. Not that many.

He settled back down and after a while *Teeku-mi* came to mind. In a matter of hours he would be confronting him. How was he going to handle this? *Teeku-mi* brought a *Jakareme* baby with him. Was he putting *Katalan* to the test? Was it going to take a miracle to have this aborigine do the right thing for these accursed people?

All of a sudden the explorer had an idea. He got up, grabbed his flashlight and hurried up to the fording spot in the brook. The night was moonless and the light kept him from slipping on the rock slime as he crossed over.

Playing the light before him, he practically ran down the main trail and up past the chief's compound to the cave entrance. He hesitated for an instant, catching his breath, and then, cupping the light with his hand, he crept inside. He could just make out two forms lying there in the dark. Mother and daughter were asleep and he had no intention of waking them. He went over to the far side of the cave and uncupping the light, drew the spotlight along the wall until he saw the purple sashes of the *masi-Jakareme*. There were at least twenty of them, all neatly folded. He scooped them and was about to head out of the cave when he caught himself. He could not leave without one last look at the woman. He directed the light on her. She was asleep, her slender form away from him. Just then little Sweet Berry beside her stirred. The explorer put the light on her and he saw the little girl flinch and turn her head away. He saw with satisfaction that *Odilia* was right where she belonged. The little girl did not wake up and he did not linger. But all the way back to his camp he pondered what he had seen. A spontaneous eye movement in her sleep. That's what it was, certainly, but it is true that since going to the cave he felt a rising tide of confidence. He could deal with *Teeku-mi,* no matter what the native's state of mind. Having the purple sashes was a brilliant inspiration. And a deep peace settled over him.

The last hours before daylight the explorer spent packing his things. He had no interest in remaining on *dundi lano* a day longer. He would introduce *Teeku-mi* to the chief, then bring this native prince to the cave. The rest he would leave to fate. What was to happen between them all after that would happen without him.

He had done what he could. He was more than ready to return to the coast and get back to his own people. Even see his son, Charlie, after these many years.

ENCOUNTER WITH *TEEKU-MI*

The explorer was up at first light. He put the purple sashes into a backpack, and with nothing else but his cane pole in hand, went out on the trail to the drop-off site. As he made his way, the pungent odor of burnt Eucalyptus grew stronger. They had kept the signal going all night, hoping for the right wind. As he neared the site, two *Chiroki* sentinels sprang out in front of him, spears pointed right at his chest. He froze as one of the natives went back to report. In an instant *Teeku-mi* appeared. He was not smiling. *Teeku-mi* waved off the guards and motioned for *Katalan* to follow him. The huge bond fire in the stone circle at the center of the site was blazing and acrid smoke billowed out, choking off any hint of fresh morning air. As he was led by the fire, he saw *Chiroki* warriors everywhere. All of them wore war paint and carried spears. There at the far edge of the rock outcropping he spotted the woman. She had a baby in her arms. In the smoke-filled early morning light he was still able to spot the purple sash of the *masi-Jakareme*.

The *Chiroki* prince turned to face *Katalan*, running his eyes up and down over him. The prince made no effort to bow. To him, nothing seemed right. *Katalan* had not brought *Lunas nili*. He was not wearing *Odilia sannu*. The two stood this way for a moment by the fire, neither of them speaking, the native searching the eyes of this *Katalan* for truth of the miracle. The explorer for his part met *Teeku-mi's* gaze with a certain sternness. Then, raising his hand, he made that ritual sign *Teeku* had taught him. As he did this, he said aloud so that all could hear, "*Katalan*-friend welcome *Teeku-mi,* son of *Matsitu.* Welcome on *dundi lano.*"

The native did not respond to any of this. "Where *Odilia sannu*?" he demanded, staring at *Katalan's* chest. For all he knew, evil spirits had vanquished the magic. But to this the explorer had the perfect answer.

"*Odilia sannu* now with daughter, *Lunas-nili,*" he said.

This disturbed the native even more. "Why with daughter?" the native demanded. Had *Odilia sannu* joined the *Jakareme*?

"*Teeku-mi* see," the explorer said. He went over to the woman at the edge of the clearing, repeated the ritual sign over her and then, with an air of ceremony, he took off her purple sash. He went back to the circle and held it high before the native prince. "*Odilia sannu* send evil spirit away," he declared. "*Jaka* no more. Evil spirit leave *dundi lano.*" And with that he threw the purple sash into the fire.

An instant murmur rose among the natives. *Teeku-mi* leapt back, gaping open-jawed. "What *Katalan* do?" he cried.

The explorer reached into his backpack. "Look," he said, taking out a single purple sash. "From *Tolani,*" he declared, holding it up to the native prince. "From wife," he said peering straight into *Teeku-mi's* bewildered face. Then he tossed it into the fire, pointing a finger as flames consumed it. "No more evil spirit on *dundi lano,*" he shouted to the warriors around him. "*Odilia sannu* remove *jaka. Jaka* no more."

Teeku-mi, dazed for a moment, sprang forward. Pointing to his eyes he cried, *"Katalan! Odilia sannu* heal *Lunas-nili?"*

The explorer held up his hand as if to stop the prince. He reached in his pack and took out the remaining purple sashes, all of them, and making like a true priest he raised them to the sky and held them there for all to see. Even God. The *Chiroki* prince froze. Here in *Katalan's* hands was the sorrow and loss of his people's long and painful history. And the eyes of this priest were shining!

"Lunas-nili?" the prince asked weakly, hands to his own eyes.

"Come, see," the explorer said. It was all he could do.

The explorer led the pack along the same single-vine trail he had traveled nine days earlier. He kept the woman close to him. She was very young and very frightened, clutching her infant to her breast. *Teeku-mi* followed behind, unsure of himself anymore, his string of painted warriors trailing him. It was broad daylight now and no one failed to see the human bones decomposing there off the path as they passed.

The explorer did not expect to meet up with any settlement folk on this rarely traveled trail, but soon they would be on the main double-vine trail and there was bound to be morning traffic, work details out to gather the days meals. Then *Teeku-mi* and his warriors will witness them, *Chiroki* men coming down the trail, groping their way, blood brothers like themselves, beardless, naked to the waist, and pitifully gaunt.

The explorer tosses Tolani's *purple sash into the flame, shouting that the curse has been lifted.*

They were not on the main, two-vine trail more than ten minutes before the explorer saw movement ahead. He turned around to *Teeku-mi* and with a commanding hand sweep ordered them into the brush just off the path. Four were coming toward them, the poles of the two in front swaying side to side. The explorer recognized Damian-Two in the lead, a stroke of wonderful luck. Hopefully by now Damian-Two knew of the explorer's identity change so that he would not be confounded.

As the party neared, the explorer made contact with his pole. As expected, everyone stopped. They went through the usual fingering of identity strings, the palming of greetings. Damian-Two, initially uncertain, felt for the beard and instantly became joyful at this unexpected encounter. All four *Jakareme* had to exchange thoughts with *hair face* friend. The explorer understood little of their palming, responding again and again merely with *good* and *thank you* signs. Finally the detail moved on and the explorer gestured the party back onto the trail. All this time no one said a word, but they had just gotten an eyeful and the explorer could not have wished for a better first encounter.

There were no further meet-ups as the explorer led them to his campsite by the pond. As they got close, all could see the bamboo groves and enclosures on the far side of the brook. Few of the *Jakareme* were about and the settlement seemed unusually quiet. They understood something new was about to happen to them, but no one knew what to expect.

At the campsite, the explorer made a comfortable place in his lean-to for the woman and her child. Feeling his authority, he instructed *Teeku-mi* to have his warriors enter the pond and remove their war paint. "No more *Jakareme*," he cried in a commanding voice. He glared around at the warriors. "No more *Jakareme*," he repeated. "Here only *children of Odilia.*" He went to the woman and took her child. Holding the infant up like an offering, he cried aloud, "*Odiliareme!*"

This was hardly like him. But this was the way it had to be, as if he had no choice in the matter, as if he were still somehow beside himself. Not wasting a moment, the explorer took the *Chiroki* prince up the trail to the fording spot in the brook. They footed their way across and moved quickly down the main trail paralleling the water. No one was out on the trail. As they came to the first of the bamboo groves on their right, the explorer stopped and let *Teeku-mi* drink in what he saw—gaunt figures under crude straw roofs set back in the groves, bent over their chores. Nothing could be more primitive, even aborigines.

Shortly the two arrived before the chief's compound. The old chief and his underlings were there in the enclosure just yards away. "Here place of *Sabuknu na Odiliareme*," the explorer explained.

The explorer began to prepare *Teeku-mi* for what would soon follow. He took off Sweet Berry's identity string and draped it around the prince's neck. Then he made a point of reaching for it and fingering its code.

"*Teeku-mi* do same with *Sabuknu*," he said.

Teeku-mi had seen enough earlier on the trail to get the drill.

Next the explorer handed *Teeku-mi* his cane pole and, placing his hand over the prince's, he tapped his own code on the ground—two short, three short, a pause and then two more short.

He looked at the native crown prince and said, "My sign. Now also *Teeku-mi* sign."

Finally, he taught *Teeku-mi* the palm greeting. This single sign would be enough to get things off on the right foot. *Tolani* would teach him beyond that.

The explorer led the *Chiroki* prince up to the dwelling. With both hands on the pole together they tapped the identity code. The chief, reacting as if he had been waiting, instantly tapped back. The explorer went in first and met the chief's extended hand. He palmed a greeting and signed the few key words *Tolani* had taught him: *New friend here. New friend want meet.* And with that the explorer took *Teeku-mi* to the chief.

Teeku-mi had learned his lesson well. He too palmed the simple greeting and then immediately felt for the chief's identity string. The chief did not reciprocate at first. The round object on *Teeku-mi's* finger had stopped him, a hard round object like the one he himself was wearing now. Instinctively, he felt for *Teeku-mi's* face. It was smooth like his own, unlike *hair face* friend. He felt for a shirt but the upper body was bare like his. Then quickly he felt for the newcomer's identity string. He knew it of course and was quick to grasp what it meant—new friend was taking the place of *hair face* friend. The chief placed both his palms on *Teeku-mi's* chest in a sign of respect. The explorer signaled to *Teeku-mi* and traced a sign on his own palm. "Sign for *thank you*," he said aloud. "*Teeku-mi* make." And this the *Chiroki* prince executed flawlessly. The chief would have palmed more but the explorer drew *Teeku-mi* off. He tapped the *goodbye* code and now took *Teeku-mi* up the path to the cave.

They stood before the cave entrance. *Teeku-mi* understood from the way *Katalan* was looking at him that the moment had come.

"*Teeku-mi* go inside," the explorer commanded. The explorer took out his flashlight, turned it on, and passed it over to the *Chiroki* prince.

"Inside wife and *Lunas-nili*," he said, and with that the explorer turned away. He hastened down the path never once looking back. And in the next minute he was on the main path heading back to his campsite. *Teeku-mi* would know the way. Primitives like him never get lost. He would come when he was ready. He would come when all that was going to happen finally happened, whatever this turned out to be.

The waiting was not easy. He tried conversation with the woman but she was too uneasy to entertain his limited *Chiroki*. The men were more relaxed without their war paint but conversation with them got nowhere also. They were all still too wary of him. He persuaded one of them to go out into the pond with his net, and the explorer built a fire thinking to cook up whatever the *Chiroki* native caught. But basically the explorer was killing time.

The wait was not long. Shortly, *Teeku-mi* came bursting into the camp and fell down at the explorer's feet. The one-time priest in that moment knew the truth. In the shining, glistening eyes of the *Chiroki* prince he saw what he had not dared to see or even dared to hope for. But there it was, no mistaking. In that face, in its marvelous, glorious radiance, the explorer too saw the miracle.

DAISY'S EPILOGUE

What we know of the explorer's story from this point on is little indeed. From some notes he left, probably written as he drifted with the current down the river, we know that when he descended *dundi lano* he went directly to the *Chiroki* village. He met with *Sabuknu* and as best he could told him all that had happened. We know also that he made a ceremonial fire in which to burn the purple sashes he had taken from the cave, and that every woman in the *Chiroki* village who bore the sash came before the fire and had her cursed sign tossed into its flames. But beyond that, all we know is that he did go back on the river.

What became of him after that is unknown. Perhaps the explorer made it back to his country, but it seems more likely he died on the river. This is what my father thought. Also, the explorer did not have the Odilia relic with him as he descended the river, so perhaps without that protection he was put to death by one of the river tribes. Perhaps, like the Jesuit priest Christopher Damian whom he came to imitate despite himself, the explorer also wound up giving his life for these people. We do not know. My father thought it telling that the explorer never showed up again in his home country, and that no one anywhere ever knew what became of him.

My father told me a few other details from the explorer's final notes. Just before the explorer went back down the Lost Mountain, the native prince, *Teeku-mi,* gave him his own family ring. And the explorer planned to give that ring to the prince's uncle, *Teeku,* who had given up his own ring at the start of this adventure. And when he reached the coast, the explorer planned to give the sturdy canoe to the boy Carlito as that would enable him to make a living, ferrying and running errands where the great river enters the bay of the port city. Most important of all, he would purchase from Carlito's father that cryptic message Christopher Damian had scrawled to *Teeku* as he lay dying. The explorer had not understood it back then, but it meant much to him now. And that is all we know about the scientist who became an explorer and more.

Just before he passed away, my father, his hands old and weak now, told me that some years after these events had taken place, the explorer's audio record and written notes had been discovered in a library in the explorer's own country. My father speculated that these items had been recovered from river tribes by coastland traders who in turn sold them to overseas tourists. Visitors to this region, I'm told, have become more frequent over the years.

But one fundamental matter in this story remained unresolved. I speak of Odilia, the saint. She, after all, lies at the very heart of this tale. Yet my father never told me who she was, whether she was real or just a figment of someone's imagination, possibly even his own. He never let on. And I suppose, being blind and deaf myself, I will never know the answer.

Author's Afterword

While I was writing this story, I had no idea of basing it on an actual saint. The relic I was depicting was entirely of an unnamed, imagined saint. But at some midway point, I thought to search the Internet to see if there indeed might be an actual saint who had dealings with the blind. What I found were two saints from centuries past, each of whom bore the name Odilia and both of whom to this day are revered as patronesses of the blind and the visually impaired. One Odilia is from the fourth century and the other from the eighth century, the former associated with Cologne and Paris, the latter with Alsace. The relics of both these saints were believed to have healing powers.

The eighth century Odilia is particularly interesting. She was born blind and, after being rejected by a royal father who could not accept a handicapped child, she hid out in a cave and was miraculously granted sight. Later she and her father were reconciled. It might be worth noting that I had conceived of this story before learning of this Odilia's history and the dramatic place in her life of a royal father and a cave.

The fourth century Odilia is the patroness of the Order of the Holy Cross (The Crosiers), an order of priests and brothers concerned with healing and most especially with problems of sight. In the 13th century, the Crosiers took Odilia as their patroness because of miraculous healings associated with her relics, relics which are venerated to this day.

Today a number of churches in the world bear the name Saint Odilia. And somehow or other, one of these Odilias (or both for that matter) found her way into this story.

I would like to leave my readers with something else that I found on the Internet, a poem that bears the title, A Common Language. The poem is by the mother of a deaf-blind daughter, written on her daughter's behalf. The authoress has graciously given me permission to quote the poem here. Clearly, this mother entered into the dark silence of her daughter's life to write these lines. In some way the poem speaks to us all.

A COMMON LANGUAGE
by Theresa Vincent

She speaks a common language
  of touch, gesture,
  a turn of the head,
  the brightness
  in her eyes.
In this silent dialect
  with the reach
  of a hand
  she asks,
  are you there?

ABOUT THE AUTHOR

Bernard Scott is a published poet, feature writer, and award-winning short story writer. *Secret of Lost Mountain* is his first novel. The author's interest in communication (and in languages most especially) becomes immediately apparent in the unfolding of this story. The tale reflects his early experience as a military linguist in a part of the world not unlike that of the novel. The author is also the developer of a high-tech computer-based translation system now available as open software on the Internet. Known as *OpenLogos*, the system is freely downloadable from the website of the German think tank, DFKI.